Of Heads&Hearts

in the

Metro

Mom, Manang Tanya, and Kristy, thank you for reading the many versions and iterations of this book, for giving me the time of day despite your busy schedules. If that isn't love, what is?

Thank you, Papa, for having always known that I'd someday publish my own book. You knew even before I graduated from grade school.

Olivia Claire, I'll always be grateful for your editorial inputs and optimism. When I doubt my writing, you lift my spirits up. Keep smiling, keep shining, Livvy!

Aiza, Tricia, Angela, Paula, Abigail, Anne, Diana, Pauline, thank you for letting me use you as guinea pigs for this project at one time or another!

Fran, your insights helped shape this book, build it up, and make it what it is today. Thank you, thank you for your amazing skill and talent. Thank you for working with me on this project. I'd never have reached this point without you.

Lanox, thank you for putting up with the crazy schedules and my insane follow-ups. Thank you for teaching me new words, style book stuff, about semicolons and quotes, and so many more!

Helena, Tere, Ebet, Junette, John Alrey, Jessel, Steph, Jenny, for enabling me to go into your worlds and develop my characters, my heartfelt thanks.

Ate Helen, for taking care of me and my family, for giving me the time I needed to write, you are the best!

Mark, for reading my books and sharing with me the male perspective, for creating such fantastic covers, for the inspiration and understanding, thank you. Most especially, for never freaking out when waking up in the middle of the night and then seeing a long-haired woman typing on a dimly lit tablet at the foot of the bed.

Caleb, you are such a great kid, letting Mom do what she loves to do. Even though Mom sometimes gets lost in her characters' worlds, your world is still Mom's favorite place to be in.

Thank you, God, for getting me through this—this awesome ride of love, of life.

For Mark,
who is my Matthew,

for Caleb,
who is my Liam,

I love you

# of Heads&Hearts
in the
Metro

THESSA LIM

CHAPTER ONE

Jazmine and the Tunnel

Snorts of laughter erupted inside the car.

Anne took her eyes off the road and stole a glance at the rearview mirror. The curls in her hair shook as she laughed noiselessly. Zara, who sat in the front seat, muffled a giggle, her eyes tearing up.

"Quiet, you two!" Laine hissed at them from the back.

Another snore came from beside Laine—Jazmine was plastered to the backseat of Anne's brand-new Prius. The hair of the *morena*[1] fell across her face as she blew out a breath.

"This is funny, but I hope she doesn't freak out when she wakes up in Batangas," Laine whispered as she leaned forward into the space between Anne and Zara.

"It wasn't my idea!" Anne piped.

Anne snuggled down in her seat and smiled. She had bought the car a week ago after her father volunteered to shoulder the down payment. Its metallic red resembled her favorite lipstick, and its contours were edgy, suiting her. She relished the smooth way the gears shifted as she sped through highways. That and the smell of new leather.

She had vowed to take her girlfriends out of town as soon as all four of them were free. It was Zara, though, who suggested

---

[1] A woman with brown complexion

that they not tell Jazmine about the trip. They told her that they would just drive around Metro Manila to break in the new car. Unfortunately for Jazmine, they picked her up right after she had shopped for groceries, and she fell asleep twenty minutes into the drive.

"It's fine. She'll be knocked out for at least another hour," Zara assured them. "Besides, we can't go out of town and leave her in the city—her and her humongous belly."

They turned to glance at Jazmine's eight-month baby bump.

Laine looked at the others. "Really? She doesn't need any medication back home?"

Zara stiffened and turned. "Not that I know of." She raised an eyebrow. "You?"

Laine shook her head.

"She'll be okay. For now, let's have some fun before the little bundle of joy arrives."

Anne's eyes met Laine's. When Zara caught this, she merely sighed. Jazmine let out another snore, but this time, the girls did not laugh.

"This is nice!" Zara squealed as she walked up to the cottage after her swim.

It was only five o'clock, and the sun was still up. She dug her toes into the fine white sand while Anne and Laine settled in the lounge chairs they had dragged along the beach to the front of their cottage.

Zara put on a black cotton tunic on top of her wet purple ruched two-piece. Anne, in her usual beach style, had on a sporty zebra-patterned high-neck bikini. Laine wore a white floral-print monokini, a green sarong wrapped around her hips.

Ten modest cottages lined the beach, each with a porch on which a coffee table rested. The beach was deserted apart from them and a little girl and a woman playing on the sand.

They arrived at the Sea Springs Resort a half hour ago. Jazmine slept through the ride. When they pulled up to the parking spot beside their cottage, with her eyes still closed, she only turned to her side and tucked a pillow beside her face. The three girls left the car's air-conditioning running and the windows down. Laine stuck a note, which said, "Beach," and had an arrow and a smiley, on Jazmine's phone.

"So, Anne, is Daniel okay that you came here without him?" Laine asked.

"Oh yeah. He didn't really say much about it."

"How are things with him?" Zara grinned at her friend.

"He's great—still romantic and sexy as ever. He takes whatever I dish out at him: drama, getting clingy. He accepts me, knows how to soothe me." Anne grinned and put on her sunglasses. "We took it slow the first three months, but now . . . he's gone where I've wanted him to go since day one."

Zara chuckled and said, "Ahh. I take it from your smile that Daniel didn't disappoint?"

"He did not," Anne replied in a singsong voice and sighed. "He's really hot! Very macho in all the right places. If there was one thing though . . ."

"What is it?" Laine asked.

"After we've made out, have gotten hot and heavy, he does this thing where he closes his eyes and grunts like . . ." Anne made a low, short guttural sound.

Zara chuckled. "Maybe he's trying to hold himself back? Before he ravages you?"

Anne mulled over this. "I don't think so."

Laine tittered. "And you were complaining that he was a take-it-slow kind of guy."

"Well, we did take our time before having sex." Anne rolled

3

her eyes, but a smile was still on her lips.

"Maybe he's just traditional," Laine suggested. "Maybe he *was* waiting for marriage before going all the way."

Anne and Zara each gave her a stern look.

"What? Some people take that seriously." Laine shrugged. "I've been waiting myself. But anyway . . . he couldn't resist you, and now you're both happy."

"It doesn't seem like he's conservative. He's Catholic but rarely goes to church. He works out regularly . . . He keeps himself in shape," Anne mused. "The other day, we were watching the latest Angelica Panganiban movie at the Cineplex . . . that movie about the mistress . . . I can't recall the title. Anyway, I thought it would turn him on right there. So I turned to hug him, put my hand on his thigh"—she leaned toward Laine and mimicked the motion on her—"and slid it up."

Laine giggled and moved out of her reach. "You didn't!"

Anne nodded, and Laine's eyes widened. "Then what happened?"

"He stopped my hand and told me, let's wait till we get to my place." Anne threw her hands up. Zara and Laine broke out laughing.

"If that were Jake, he'd have slid my hand all the way up to where it counts." Zara grinned. "Oh, stop blushing, Laine. We're in our midtwenties."

"That was pretty gentlemanly of Daniel," Laine contended.

Anne simpered as her friends argued about her man.

Jazmine woke up and looked around the car. Her eyebrows furrowed. The last thing she remembered was the car passing by Bicutan along the Metro Manila Skyway.

The light streaming in the windows was dark orange; the

sun was setting outside.

"Oooh! Fruit shakes! Thank you, *Kuya*!"[2] Zara's voice flitted in from outside.

Jazmine panicked and felt her belly. Relieved when she felt the baby moving inside, she grabbed the note. Her heart raced. She got out of the car and walked toward the beach.

A sight to behold: her three friends on lounge chairs on the beach, sipping fruit shakes.

"You girls have no shame!" Jazmine wailed at them as she stared out at the long stretch of sand and the sea in front of her. Her eyes and nostrils flared.

Three heads snapped back to look at her. Three faces tensed. Laine jumped up and rushed over to Jazmine.

"Jazmine, surprise! We're having your baby shower here at the beach!" Laine was all smiles at Jazmine, but her voice came out all pitchy.

"Where are we?" Jazmine demanded.

"At the Sea Springs Resort . . . in Batangas," Laine answered sheepishly.

"Batangas? How can you take me all the way here? Are we going back soon?" Jazmine turned and looked at the cottage, the door was ajar, and she spotted Anne's bag on the table on the porch. She turned to look at them again. "Did you bring my things?"

"We got you day and night clothes . . ."

"What about my baby books? I have to read to the baby tonight. My vitamins? Bolster pillow?"

"Umm . . ." Laine cringed.

"*And* I have to meet with Sue tomorrow! How can you do this without telling me?"

---

[2] A title for a male who is older

"Jaz, calm down. We just wanted to go before the baby arrives. We won't be able to do this much then," Zara tried with a soothing tone.

"*You* won't be able to do this much? No, you mean, *I* won't be able to do this much. While you guys will get on with your carefree ways, vacations, and nights out, I'll be stuck at home with the baby alone." Jazmine was close to tears—they swore she could be set off sobbing with a snap of a finger those days.

"Jaz, we'll be with you all the way. We're not like Braden, you know," Anne pitched in.

"Gals, I can't do this right now. I've so much to prepare for." Jazmine sobbed. "I've to watch those labor videos and practice my Lamaze breathing."

"Jaz, come on." Laine hugged her.

Anne and Zara walked toward her too.

"Group hug!"

Jazmine pushed them away, still crying. "Hold on. I think I'm hyperventilating. Oh my gosh." Suddenly she froze, and her eyes widened like saucers. "Oh my God!"

Jazmine eased down to the sand, holding on to Laine.

"What's wrong with her?" Anne asked, pulling at Zara's wrist.

"I-I don't know!" Zara looked at Jazmine.

Laine knelt beside Jazmine and held her. Suddenly, Laine felt the sand around her knees become wet.

She gasped. "Gals, I think her water just broke!"

"What do you mean her water just broke? She's only eight months pregnant! Don't you need nine months for that?" Anne cried.

Jazmine clutched her belly. "I'm thirty-six weeks pregnant! I can go . . . anytime. Ahh! What was that?" She paled and looked up at her friends. "Aaahh! Why the hell is it hurting?

Shouldn't I have some time," she grunted, "after my water breaks? Am I in labor already?"

When Jazmine began to writhe, and her breaths began to come in rapid succession, the three other girls grabbed one another's hands.

"Shit!"

Zara hastily scanned the area; they would be lucky if there were a doctor in one of the beachside cottages. She closed her eyes and steadied herself.

"Okay, gals, this is what we'll do. I'll get her mobile and call her OB. Maybe she knows a doctor here. Or a midwife. Anne, ask the receptionist for directions to the nearest hospital." Anne nodded and clapped her hands, like she would for an obstacle course. "Laine, stay with Jaz. I'll pack up our things. We're going to the hospital!"

There was a frenzy as Jazmine's friends scurried about. Laine led her to one of the lounge chairs. Jazmine sat down and tried to drag her mind away from the pain. Hoping that it would help to look at the sea, she looked around her, and calm came over her.

This place is beautiful.

The sun was setting in a picture-perfect way. The waves twinkled and crashed against the shore. Coconut palms swayed along with the soft breeze. A little girl was running around a sandcastle while a woman prodded her on with cheers.

Zara was on the phone. "Dr. Nats," she said, trying to keep calm, "it seems that Jazmine's water has broken . . . Is it early? She's in pain. We're now in Batangas, so we can't get to you."

The doctor barked that Jazmine should not have been traveling but then gave Zara an obstetrician to contact.

As the doctor spoke, Zara scoured the cottage, grabbing

what she could find, rushing to drop them at the car trunk, and tripping over her feet a few times.

When Anne came back, she reported, "The receptionist gave me the directions to the hospital. I also already checked us out."

"I got the local doctor. She's got a midwife in the hospital. She'll come in as soon as she can," Zara announced from the porch.

"Laine, let's go!" Anne called out.

Anne hurried to help Jazmine up. "Come on, girl. Let's do this shit!"

In a few minutes, Anne was speeding through the provincial roads. Zara was on the phone with the local doctor again.

"Jaz, she said it's normal to have contractions after your water breaks."

Jazmine was now sweating, going through the onset of labor. "Uh-huh. Can you ask her how to stop the pain then?"

"She said to take slow and deep breaths."

"If something happens to Jaz, I'll never forgive myself," Laine cried.

"This was my idea!" Zara buried her face in her hands.

"Suck it up, you two!" Anne hissed. "From here on, only Jaz gets to whine. Now, according to this map, just two more turns and we should be at the hospital."

The midwife was there to greet them at the hospital reception and led them to a labor room. Zara did the registration as the midwife gave Jazmine instructions.

"Count the duration between the contractions," she said. "I'll check in on you every fifteen minutes."

After the midwife left, Laine asked, "Jaz, are you okay?

How are you feeling?"

Jazmine sat on the bed, sweating and getting paler and paler.

"What do you think?" Jazmine hissed in between labored breaths, but her eyes were alive with purpose.

"We're so sorry about this. Please forgive us."

"If Liam and I live through this, let me get back to you on that."

"You're naming him Liam?"

"Yes." Jazmine then grunted as a contraction tore through her. "Like a lion!"

"A lion? What lion?" Anne asked Laine, who shrugged back.

The girls took turns massaging Jazmine's lower back, wiping her face, getting a fresh hot compress, and helping her to more comfortable positions. After three hours of monitoring the labor, the midwife did another check on how dilated Jazmine was.

"Shit!" Anne covered her mouth with her hand and mumbled, "She looks like she's in so much pain. I-I . . ." Anne turned around and headed for the only couch in the room.

Laine gulped as she spied the smears of blood on the bed. "Sh-she's strong. She's g-going to be fine."

Zara grabbed Laine's hand and whispered, "I'm about to freak out, Laine. I never expected . . . this. Stop me from freaking out?"

Laine squeezed her hand. "They're going to b-be fine."

"She's in the final stages of labor. The doctor is already in, so I'll take her to the delivery room. You girls will have to wait in the visitors' area," the midwife announced, and she rolled Jazmine's bed out of the room.

The three girls cheered Jazmine on, but as soon as she was out of sight, what little that was left of their bravado deserted them. They sank onto the couch, heaved sighs, and uttered prayers for their friend. It had been the most intimate and scary night of their lives.

CHAPTER TWO

After the Tunnel

Jazmine drifted awake. Her hand reached for her stomach, but she felt only her own flesh there. Images of the night before flashed through her mind: the doctor encouraging her to push during her contractions, the midwife pressing down on her stomach to help the baby come out, and then, her baby. Her baby was held by the doctor as he bellowed his first cry. They had let her hold him as mother and child were wheeled into a hospital room. Her friends had come to her room with expectant grins and had taken turns holding the little one. Sometime in the middle of the night, a nurse dropped by to remind them that visiting hours were over and only one visitor could stay overnight. The nurse urged her to rest and then took Liam to the nursery.

Jazmine tried to move, but her lower back was stiff. She tried to push herself up, but her arms were tired.

What had I been doing during the delivery?

She tried to speak but could only cough.

"Zara . . . ," she called when she saw Zara lying down on the couch by the window.

Zara woke up with a start. "Jaz! How are you feeling?"

Jazmine coughed. "I need water."

Zara poured water into a cup on the bedside table and handed it to her friend.

"Liam is still at the nursery. The nurse said he should be back here by six. Some newborn tests they have to do." Zara beamed at her. "You did such a great job! He's perfect." She took the cup from Jazmine and refilled it. "Anne and Laine went back to Manila to get some clothes for you and him."

"Thanks, you gals. I can't believe I survived last night." Her face scrunched, and she cried. She reached for Zara's hand, but her own hand trembled as she moved. "Please don't leave me . . . I'm s-scared."

"Jaz, we're here for you. We're so sorry we didn't tell you and brought you here. It was selfish. If-if anything had happened . . ."

Jazmine nodded through her tears. "I'm just glad you're here. Even if we were back in the city, I don't know what I would've done if you gals weren't around."

Zara slid her arm around Jazmine's shoulders. "Jaz, can you please never ever doubt us? We're tight, like sisters." She glanced at the door and back at her friend. "Do you want me to get Liam?"

Jazmine nodded and smiled. "Yes, please."

Jazmine held Liam and thanked God that he did not have his father's looks yet. Her baby was perfect. She felt sad that Braden had not been there to experience this. But now, Liam was *hers,* not *theirs*, but only *hers*.

"Jaz, I can't go through with this. It scares the hell out of me. I'm too young to be involved in something like this."

"Braden, I can't do this without you." Jazmine felt a weight settle in her heart. Suddenly she felt cold.

"And I can't do this. I can't take responsibility for this."

"Braden, please! This is our baby!" Jazmine's voice hitched. *"My family—"*

"They'll want me to look after them too. It's too heavy for me.

Too big."

"Please don't do this . . ."

"Sorry, Jaz. Really, I am. But . . . goodbye, Jaz."

They had been together for two years; it seemed like a dream. They would date every weekend. And even though she was demure, she learned to kiss passionately and hold him close. After weeks of coaxing, then increased intimacy, she was finally seduced.

Jazmine wanted him to be the man she would marry so that she would only ever be with one man her entire life. Braden was not known for steadfastness, but he made her laugh, gave her flowers when there was an occasion, and accompanied her wherever she wanted to go.

He left her when she was five months pregnant.

A month before Braden abandoned her, she went home to Legazpi on the eight-hour rail trip to the eastern end of Luzon. The day was hot and humid, and her hormones . . . The spicy *dilis*[3] her seatmate was eating reeked and made her want to throw up—it was not dried fish really; it smelled like bloody, dead fish. The chickens clucking among the belongings of another passenger smelled to her like what they were—poultry and their feces. Braden could not join her then; he had to work overtime, he had said. Looking back now, she was not sure he had been at the office at all.

"What? You're pregnant? What's going to happen to us?" Jazmine's mother demanded, slapping her hand on the dining table. "Who will send your sister to school? She's still in high school!" Her mother stood with a hand on her hip and a glare on her face.

Jazmine's mouth dropped open, but she quickly closed it.

---

[3] Dried anchovies with red coating, usually served spicy or sweet and spicy

No care, no courtesy. The selfishness laid bare.

"Well, I haven't really thought about how much the baby will cost . . . not yet," Jazmine mumbled.

"Does Braden have a good job? How much does he make a month?" her father added and stared at her from his seat. "I welcomed that shameless twit to our home, and this is what he does to me?"

"How can you do this to us?" Her mother threw her hands up in the air. "Can we still expect any help from you?"

She did not even notice that her daughter was sweating, her legs swollen from the trip, and her feet red since she walked the thousand meters from the main road to the house.

Jazmine could only cringe as the implications of the pregnancy on her family dawned on her. Out of the corner of her eye, Jazmine saw her sister, Christine, peeking down at them from the top of the stairs.

What happens to Christine from now on . . . I can't think of it.

Since Jazmine had started working in Manila after university, she earned enough to look after herself and send money for her sister's education as well as her parents' monthly expenses. Six months after she began sending money home, her mother stopped working at the factory, and her father was not so concerned anymore about looking for jobs or keeping them.

At that moment, as Jazmine gazed at her beautiful boy, her Liam, the troubles of the past months all seemed worth the hurt. She had no idea how to take care of a baby. She had read things in books and online, but she was going to have to wing it. She was certain her three girlfriends had no idea either. But by any means, she was going to take care of this baby and give him a handsome future.

CHAPTER THREE
Zara and the Break

Three weeks passed since Liam's birth. In those weeks, the girls had grappled with learning how to care for a newborn. That and Jazmine's special attention to Liam's laundry and diaper changing. During the weekdays, one of them went to Jazmine's home, dropping off packed food, letting her get in the shower, or joining her for dinner. Over the weekends, they ran errands, played with Liam, and, in the rare times the opportunity presented itself, lazed in front of the television in her apartment.

This Thursday morning, Zara prepared to fly to Cebu to meet Jake. The girls were too busy attending to Liam that she had to take a taxi by herself to the airport.

Jake was her boyfriend of two and a half years. They met while they were at the university, but it was not until they were working that they got to know each other. Jake used to work at an investment bank in the building right next to Zara's office. They bumped into each other on the street one time.

"I'm on my way to get lunch. Want to join me?" he had said.

She had smiled and nodded wide-eyed. He was wearing black, and good-looking men dressed in black always made her bite her lower lip. A week later, they started dating.

A year passed, and Jake received a job offer in Singapore. Without a second thought, he grabbed the opportunity and relocated. At first, Zara encouraged him, letting him cut Skype dates short or miss her birthday when he was busy abroad, but then later found out that she missed the physical company, the late-night dates, and the hours-long conversations. They only saw each other every three months or less often than that. During those times, Jake either flew to Manila or arranged for both of them to fly for a vacation.

The previous week, Jake had to work late hours in the nights, and on the few hours when he was free to chat online, she was caught up in a meeting or a social engagement. She had lashed out at him and demanded that he relocate back to Manila. Jake pragmatically pointed out why he could not do so, and then she also pragmatically pointed out why she could not move to Singapore. They had reached an impasse. Feeling that she should be reasonable about things, she dropped the subject then.

Jake was waiting for her at the Cebu Airport. They boarded the car he hired to take them to the port where they would catch a ferry to Bantayan Island.

Jake nudged her chin. "Are you okay? You've been quiet."

"I'm often quiet." She smiled and shrugged. "Just a little tired." It did not help that she missed a night's sleep when she took her turn helping Jazmine with Liam a couple of nights before.

She brightened the mood by telling him about all the stuff they could do at the island. She had done her homework and wanted to cover the top five highlights . . . at the least.

As she filled him in about a cave they should visit, his mobile rang. When he glimpsed who the caller was, he lifted a hand and answered the phone. Her mouth hung open as she paused midsentence.

During the two-hour drive to the ferry port, Jake's mobile sounded every now and then. Realizing that they were not going to be alone this weekend, she turned her gaze out the window, taking in the different towns they passed. Zara was a writer at a travel magazine and was used to going out of town around the country. The sights were familiar, as provincial towns usually looked the same, and she liked observing people as they went about their daily business.

She smiled weakly as she watched an old man pushing a rickety wooden cart filled with coconuts. He crossed the road as a *jeepney*[4] stopped at the side. An old woman, lugging a live chicken with its legs bound with rope, boarded the vehicle even though it was already full. Finding out that she could no longer squeeze in, she sat at the edge of the *jeepney* and loudly tapped on its side to signal the driver to move on. When the engine roared to continue the trip, kids who just made purchases at a nearby *sari-sari*[5] store made a play of racing after it.

The sun was already setting when they arrived. They were staying at the newest resort on the island. Two-story Mediterranean-style villas, painted with pastel colors, stood all over the Liberty Lodge Resort property. Orange, yellow, and blue tiles that festooned the floor and the tops and bottoms of the walls reminded Zara of pictures of Gaudi's Park Güell in Barcelona.

Once they entered their room and dropped their bags onto

[4] A vehicle used as public transport in the Philippines, originally made from U.S. military jeeps left over from World War II and well-known for their flamboyant decoration and crowded seating

[5] A small store that sells cheap household and kitchen items

the floor, Jake set his phone aside on the bedside table. He grabbed Zara's waist and started kissing her on the lips and neck.

"Jake . . ." Zara gasped and chuckled as he playfully nuzzled her ear.

"I missed you." Jake stared into Zara's eyes as he cupped the back of her head and kissed her fully on the lips.

He brushed a hand down her long dark hair and smiled. When he ran his hands all over her slim body, his breathing quickened, and his cheeks flushed. She took in the hungry look on his handsome face and his toned body clad in preppy beach attire, and breathed, "I missed you too."

Zara wanted to talk about the thought that had been nagging her, but before she could say anything, Jake was kissing her with urgency. She felt her body melt against his, and she pushed away whatever betraying notion her mind held.

That would have to wait.

She was going to have these few days with Jake.

The next day, Jake and Zara made plans to explore the island. Even though Jake joined Zara in swimming and lounging by the beach, he only did so in the morning. When afternoon came, he excused himself from snorkeling to return to his laptop.

Late in the afternoon of Saturday, Zara strolled around the small town of Bantayan by herself. Jake had to respond to some emails and had stayed in their room. She walked barefoot along the shores of their resort. The breeze was cool. When the sun began to set, Zara stopped and sat down on the fine white sand. She stared at the orange hues on the sky and hugged herself.

After a few minutes, she heard footsteps pad on the sand.

Jake plopped himself down beside her.

"I saw you from upstairs," he explained.

She nodded but did not meet his eyes. He wrapped an arm around her shoulders and moved closer.

When he squeezed her shoulder, Zara finally spoke, "The tide was pretty high this morning. The water was great. I wish we had taken that *bangka*[6] ride around the island."

Jake pursed his lips. "That would've been nice."

"But impossible."

With all the things you have to do.

Jake watched her with a puzzled look on his face. He shook his head and stared at the sky with a frown. Suddenly the smells of the salty sea, the heat and sweat on their burnt skin, and the sunblock made her heady.

"Jake, I wanted to talk about us."

He grunted. "Last we talked, we couldn't reach an agreement."

"I know, but shouldn't we? I honestly don't know how much more of the long distance I can handle."

"Have you changed your mind?"

"No."

"I haven't changed mine either. We've got to work with what we have now. People have done this before. It's not impossible, hon."

Zara clenched her fists but only heaved a sigh. This was what he said the last time as well. "Then I guess you don't really care that this is killing me inside."

"Zara, of course I care, but we have to take advantage of opportunities on hand."

Zara swallowed. Her mind reeled over the fact that she was

---

[6] A dugout canoe with outriggers and a roof of bamboo

now seriously considering ending their relationship this very weekend.

As the moon peeked at them from behind the grey clouds, Jake and Zara sat on the wicker rattan furniture on the veranda of their villa. Zara sulked as she curled up on her side of the bench. She had barely spoken since their conversation at the beach. Her dinner had gone almost untouched.

He glanced at her, considering her for a moment. "Did you enjoy this weekend? You look great in your tan."

She shrugged.

He smiled. "In fact, not just great. Sexy would be a better word." He reached for her and pulled her up. "Come here." He leaned forward and bit at her earlobe.

She flinched and pushed him away. "Stop it."

He frowned. "What's wrong?"

"You probably talked more to your boss than you did to me this weekend." She inched away. "And this was supposed to be *our* time."

His shoulders slumped. "I'm sorry . . . It's pretty hectic at the office nowadays. Everybody's tense about a divestment deal."

"B-but I'm here. I'm making time for you . . ." She looked him in the eyes. "We've barely talked these last weeks. I feel like, like we're drifting apart."

"No, we're not." He shook his head. "Things are the same as before. Nothing's changed with me."

"No, you're different," she insisted and huffed out a breath. "You've learned how to zone me out. When you attend to your calls and numbers and papers, you don't see me anymore."

He sighed and rubbed the back of his neck. "That's not true. I . . ."

He can't even explain it.

Her body shook.

He sighed. "Hon, just come here."

He touched her arm, but she slapped his hand away.

"Don't." He could barely hear her when she whispered, "Years ago, I promised myself I'd never love anybody more than he loved me . . . And yet, here I am with you."

He seethed and stood up. "Now that's unfair! How can you question me like this?"

She threw him a dark look. "Don't think you haven't given me any reason to—"

"This is low, Zara," he growled. "You should know how much I love you—"

Her chest ached. How she wanted to believe him. But every week since she asked him to come back, every week that he spent away from her made her wonder.

"Why does she have to call you when she knows you're away on vacation?"

"Who?"

"Your boss."

He shrugged. "I'm just moving up. She trusts me."

On a particularly lonely night, Zara had googled his boss and found her on LinkedIn and Facebook. The woman was probably several years his senior, but she was still a pretty thing. Pretty and single from what Zara managed to dig up.

"Is there somebody else?" Zara breathed. This time, she could not look at his face. Her eyes watered as she waited for his answer.

He cursed. "Don't pit me against your exes."

"Then why have you changed? Years ago, you said you just wanted to try working abroad. You said a couple of years was all you wanted. Why haven't you talked about coming back?"

21

He shook his head and only continued to glare at her. "Did you even hear yourself just now? Do you know how hurtful your words are? You accuse me of something your mind only made up, because you let yourself feed on your regrets."

Her palms sweated and turned cold. She braced herself for what was to come.

I can't help it. I can't fix this part of me . . . And the distance between us is only making it worse.

With her eyes closed, she said, "Let's end this now. I can't do this anymore . . . I've been thinking about it since you last went away." Her voice cracked, and she opened her eyes. "I . . . I'm not strong enough to wait for you *every* time. And you . . . you don't want to come back, which makes me feel that I'm never going to be good enough for you."

"So what you're saying is, I should go back to Manila or else we're over?"

Ugly and selfish. But I have to be now to protect myself.

She looked at the ground, her shoulders slumped.

He cursed and walked out on her.

When she woke up the next day, Jake had already packed and gone. He left a note saying he was taking the first ferry off the island and she should take the ferry before noon so that she could catch her flight back to Manila. Zara cried when the reality of the breakup sank in.

He didn't even fight for us.

After Jake came back to their villa the previous night, he did not talk to her and had a stony look on his face the entire time. He even slept on the rattan sofa.

Zara packed her things and walked the walk of shame to the reception. She found out that they had been checked out already. When asked if she needed two seats on the shuttle van that would bring her to the Bantayan port, she looked away and said she only needed one.

After the ferry ride back to the mainland, a rental car picked her up at the port to bring her to the city. The driver chatted with her eagerly, trying out his Tagalog with her, but Zara could barely smile at him.

Remembering Cebu's finest, Zara asked the driver to stop by a local market for the famous Cebu *lechon*[7] and *chorizo*.[8] She might just gripe about her heartbreak over all the sweet *chorizo* she could get.

Does chorizo taste good with vodka—lots and lots of vodka?

---

[7] A suckling pig that is roasted

[8] Pork sausage in natural casings made from pig intestines

CHAPTER FOUR
Anne and the Cranny

"Your core is not aligned," Zack, her personal trainer, scolded.

"And you're busting my ass!" Anne wailed at him as she grunted to correct her form and continued her set of squats.

"So that your ass will look like a work of art." Zack winked at her as sweat rolled down all over her body.

"Are you saying it still isn't?" she hissed in between breaths as the barbell on her shoulders bore down on her even more.

Ten more squats to go. Shit.

"I'm saying it can be finer. Fourteen more."

"What? Nine left!"

"Thirteen more 'cause you griped."

She adjusted her fingers around the bar and flipped him off. They both laughed. Anne did thirteen more to finish the set and then sank onto the floor.

"Water break. Then we have to do dumbbells."

Anne groaned but knew this was why she maintained a personal trainer at the gym. She needed somebody to keep her committed to her program.

Anne had kept her "baby fat" all the way until her high school years. When she slimmed down while studying at the university, she expanded her wardrobe. People began looking her way when she walked into a room, and she learned to speak up more often. With her father's generous allowance, she began hanging out with the in-crowd, dining at fancy restaurants, and partying at the hippest bars. She vowed then to keep her body as fit as she could.

When she availed of a free weight training trial after she started working, that vow she made years ago took on a life of its own. She could not stay away from the gym for longer than three days—unless on vacation. And even then, she would pay a visit to the hotel facility. If it smelled right, she could stay for hours. She had gone to the same gym even though new hipper ones had sprung about the metro as fitness became a trendy interest among young urbanites. Why Zack, her personal trainer since she started, continued to stay with the same gym for years always puzzled her though. She was certain that the newer ones gave better pay and had better facilities for trainers to work with. She reckoned, if he transferred to another gym, she would follow suit.

"Anything happening this weekend?" Zack asked her as they headed for the water dispenser.

"Yeah. My boyfriend is coming over for dinner with my parents tonight."

"Meet the parents? Getting serious there?" He smirked. Anne had never been in a long-term relationship. The longest relationship she had lasted only eight months.

"I've reached that age when I need to start introducing my guy to my parents."

"Is there such a thing?" He chuckled.

"I think so. It's so that they'll take me seriously. They'll think I'm trying to settle down."

"And are you?"

"No." She grinned at him.

He laughed at this and threw her towel at her face.

One of the most beautiful china sets they owned was meticulously laid out on the dining table. The plates and bowls were all lined along the rim with gold coating. The silver spoons, forks, and other cutleries all had a similar lustrous yellow coating on the edge of their handles.

Anne squirmed. Her parents usually ordered the maids to get the fanciest dining ware when they aimed to either impress or intimidate the guest. Since it was her boyfriend who was coming over tonight, she guessed it was the latter.

Daniel was wearing a crisp blue-collared shirt that highlighted his broad chest and handsome face. His look for the evening made him fit in with the rest of the dining party. Anne's father, Raul, was dressed in a collared white cotton Lacoste shirt. Her mother, Priscilla, had on a tailored ecru Kate Spade dress. Her eldest sister, Elizabeth, was seated across her mother with her husband, John, both looking pristine in their white ensemble: a petite flute sleeve dress and a crisp shirt with cream chinos. Her second-eldest sister, Catherine, donned a black suit—no . . . a black pencil dress. Anne, clad in a yellow sundress with floral prints, was sitting beside her mother.

"Daniel works in the business development of H&M in Makati." Anne beamed at Daniel. When her parents' expressions did not change, she realized she would have to make her sales pitch better. Good thing, selling was what she did for a living. "He's the youngest in their team, but he's already one of the senior executives. H&M has grown quite well in Manila."

"Is H&M that Swedish clothing store with a mass market?" Priscilla looked at Raul, her eyebrows furrowed.

Anne fumed.

Her parents had loved her brother-in-law, John, right away

because they had business relations with his parents. Knowing that Elizabeth would join the business if they married, they had been all the more enthusiastic about him. Equally so, John's parents loved Elizabeth. With a master's degree in business administration under her belt, she plunged into John's family business right away after the wedding. The in-laws would have claimed her as their biological child if they could.

Catherine was a corporate lawyer who spent days and nights at the office. She made Anne squirm with her knowledge of the news, social events, and business. Their parents never pried into her dating life nor checked what she was eating or how work was. Her debate-like stance in things she believed in was probably warning enough. Their respect for her only grew more when she topped the bar exams. Anne would not be surprised if she started her own firm in the future.

Meanwhile, Anne was a sales executive at a European IT firm. No academic honors, no business to claim, an employee. To her parents, she was just somebody who marketed things to companies and begged them to purchase the firm's software. No matter how hard she worked, and even if she had already won several accounts for her firm, her parents had yet to acknowledge her career. All this infuriated her.

Perhaps introducing Daniel would make them see me in a new light, a more grown-up light.

Raul took a sip from his wineglass before answering. "Yes, honey. I think that's the one." He winked at Anne and said to his wife, "You liked their suit collection."

"So you've shopped there before," Anne spoke matter-of-factly, the pitch of her voice controlled.

"How did you two meet?" Priscilla brushed off her comment with a wave of her hand.

"He's a friend of Jamie, my officemate."

"And . . . ?"

"And we were out for drinks once, and Daniel happened to be there. Jamie introduced us."

"So you met at a bar?" Priscilla squirmed at the thought.

"Yes, but he's more of an acquaintance of a colleague." Anne finally snapped, "Don't make it sound that way."

"Don't bark at me, Anne. I'm trying to get to know the situation."

"Jamie and I went to the same college at the University of the Philippines," Daniel offered, rubbing Anne's hand under the table.

"Ahh . . ." Priscilla smiled and peered at him more closely. She apparently appreciated his educational background. "Your name is Daniel de Sola, right? Are you in any way related to Dominic de Sola?"

Daniel cleared his throat and avoided the suddenly intrigued gazes of Anne's parents. "Yes, he's my father."

Anne breathed, and her shoulders lifted. "Have you done business with him before, Mom?" she asked.

"Yes, we have," Priscilla answered but looked up to the ceiling, an eyebrow raised, trying to recall something. "He imports some of the hardware we need to fashion our jewelry. He has some of the best quality materials." Anne's parents were in the jewelry business.

"Ahh, then our parents know each other." Anne beamed at Daniel.

He nodded but avoided her eyes.

From there, Priscilla inquired a lot more of Daniel. He answered her questions politely, but his answers got more and more clipped over the hour.

After dinner, as Daniel was in the foyer, getting ready to

leave, Anne slid her arms around his waist. The large molave door loomed behind them, foreboding of a brief rendezvous that evening. Anne tugged him back toward the living room, where her parents and sisters had gathered for hot chocolate and chitchat, but he did not budge. She spread her palms over his chest and caressed it, throwing him a look while biting her lower lip. She grinned up at him—mischief all over her face—but he only raised an eyebrow in amusement.

"Do you want to hang out? Maybe we can go somewhere?" Anne suggested.

"I think I'll head home. I've got an early meeting tomorrow."

She pouted.

"Some other time." He smiled and gave her a kiss on the forehead.

On the forehead? I want the works tonight: cheeks, lips, neck, and chest. Anywhere further sounds even better.

When he did not kiss her again, she retorted, "And how come I've never met your family?"

"They're always so busy."

"Your parents suck."

He smiled. "You can meet my cousin Ronnie sometime."

"Is he the one who kicked your Labrador when you were little and made you cry?"

"Yeah, the very one. And tickled me until I peed." He chuckled to himself and then looked at her. "Good night, babe. I'll see you on Friday, okay?"

"Fine. See you then." She pouted in the most ungracious manner she could. "But I need more kisses."

When he leaned down to kiss her cheek, she pulled his face to hers and gave him a smack right on the lips. She wanted to deepen the kiss, but he cupped her face and held her back.

"Your parents might be offended if they find us like this in your home."

Anne let out a heavy sigh, and her shoulders slumped. "I don't care."

Daniel chuckled. "Well, I care. I might want to visit again."

She beamed at him. He laid a kiss goodbye on her lips.

When Anne walked back into the living room, she glared at her mother.

"Mom, what was with the fifty questions?" Anne interrupted the conversation as Catherine explained the latest news on the Senate's probe into a corruption scandal.

Catherine stopped midsentence and cleared her throat. "So, I guess we're talking about that." She turned to her mother and smiled. "Mom?"

Priscilla sighed and looked up at her youngest daughter, who stood in front of them with a hand on her hip. "You brought him here for us to meet him. I wanted to know him better. I was giving him due attention."

Anne rolled her eyes. "You could've been more pleasant."

Priscilla shushed Anne. "Men have to endure these uncomfortable situations. It's natural for parents of ladies to be inquisitive."

Anne raised an eyebrow. "I don't remember John being questioned as much."

John shifted in his seat but remained silent. Elizabeth merely smiled at the mention of her husband and waited for Priscilla to answer the rebuttal.

Before Priscilla could say anything, Raul pulled Anne by the wrist and made her sit down on the couch. "Come here, dear. Have some cocoa. I got your favorite one."

Anne frowned as her father slid an arm around her

shoulders. "I thought we'd run out. Where'd you get this?" she asked.

Raul glanced at the cup in his hand. "Bought it at Rustan's."

"Dad, I told you I buy this in bulk, so I can get it cheaper," Anne groaned.

Raul chuckled. "I just bought a few packs. Can't I buy something for my little cuddly bear?"

Anne groaned. Elizabeth and Catherine snickered.

Ugh!

CHAPTER FIVE

The Feasting on Lechon

The sun had set that Friday afternoon. The four girls were at Jazmine's apartment enjoying the *lechon* Zara brought, while Liam napped in the bedroom. Jazmine's apartment was a modest one-bedroom old unit in the outskirts of Mandaluyong City. The fittings and furniture had scratches, chipped-off corners, and tears here and there, but the earthy colors that adorned the place, along with Jazmine's upkeep, still made a visitor feel like there were chocolate crinkles baking in the oven.

"I'm breaking open the dessert. It's an English Battenberg cake," Laine announced and laid a glass pot on the table.

"Laine, you're a great cook. But your baking . . ." Zara peered in to get a better look. "It looks like it's about to cave in."

Laine pouted at her. "Even if it caves, it might taste good. See, it's pink and yellow on the inside. Very pretty." She took out a knife and cut four slices from the cake and served them.

"Gals, I want to thank you for always coming over." Jazmine looked each of her friends in the eyes. "Every day since Liam was born, one of you has been over here."

"Well, Zara has us on a schedule," Anne grumbled, picking up a crispy piece of pork skin and popping it into her mouth.

Jazmine's eyes widened, and she gawked at Zara.

"Seriously?"

"Yes, Jaz. Somebody has to wield an iron hand around here and make sure everybody helps out. With you breastfeeding, making sure Liam's *this* is clean and Liam's *that* is clean, it's *moi*." Zara pointed to her chest and winked at her.

Jazmine sniffed and squeezed Zara's hand. "And, Anne, thanks for convincing your parents to loan me *Ate*[9] Helen when I go back to work. I'll definitely pay Ate for her help. It's the least I can do."

"Not necessary, but I'm sure she'd like that. Do that instead of sending money to your unsupportive family," Anne grumbled.

"I can't just let my sister down, you know. Christine has been doing so well at school." Jazmine hesitated. "I sent her some money in our joint account and saw that she'd withdrawn a part of it. But she never sent me an email nor a text. I think . . . our parents have forbidden her to talk to me."

Laine made a face and inquired, "Are you going to keep sending money to your parents?"

"I don't have enough to give them. Maybe only during the summer when Christine doesn't have school."

Suddenly Jazmine's phone rang. Three short rings before Jazmine let her eyes drop and scan the screen. When Jazmine saw who was calling, her body tensed and her eyes widened.

"It's Tita[10] Fiona," Jazmine breathed. She plucked the phone with both hands.

Anne took another piece of *lechon* from the serving platter. "Who's that?"

---

[9] Used to address older women as a sign of respect
[10] Aunt; also used to address older unrelated women who are accorded the same respect as one's parents

Jazmine gulped. "Braden's mother."

Zara made a face and mumbled, "Word's gone out. About time."

"I don't want to talk to her," Jazmine groaned and frowned. "How could she have known? I only texted Braden—"

"You texted him?" Anne growled.

Jazmine stared at the screen where the name "Fiona Palma" blinked and prodded her to pick up.

"I had to," she argued. "He's Liam's father."

"Jaz?" Laine gestured to the phone. "Are you going to take the call or not?"

Jazmine's finger shook as she tapped on the green button to answer. She walked away from the table.

"H-hi, Tita," she greeted.

The once-familiar voice made her insides clench. "Hi, Jazmine. How are you?"

They made the customary chitchat, asked each other how they were, and said they were fine.

Why is she calling?

"Jazmine, I heard about what happened . . . ," Fiona started.

"W-what are you talking about, Tita?" Jazmine pursed her lips.

"That—" Fiona sighed. "That you got pregnant before you and my son broke up. And that you'd given birth . . ."

A long silence followed.

Jazmine took a deep breath. "That's true."

When Fiona did not say anything, Jazmine spoke up, "The baby's healthy . . . Is that why you called?"

Fiona let out another sigh. "Can I meet him? Or her?"

Jazmine thought she heard a catch in the woman's voice.

Oh man.

"The baby's a boy . . . I-I think that should be fine."

Jazmine cringed.

It'd be very, very awkward, but it would be fine.

"I . . ." The break in Fiona's voice was audible this time. "I want to help you . . . to help care for him."

When the call ended, the cold had left her hands, but they still trembled. Jazmine turned around to face her friends. Zara was talking about the breakup with Jake.

Laine looked up. "Jaz, what did she say? Are you okay?"

"Tita wants to help look after Liam," Jazmine answered, her breathing evening out. "She's coming here next week to meet him."

"I say no," Anne declared and crossed her arms. "If Braden doesn't want anything to do with Liam, his family shouldn't either."

Jazmine let out a breath and sat down. "I don't know, Anne . . . I could really use the help. She said she can help me support him." Jazmine looked at Laine and Zara. "What do you girls think?"

Anne huffed out a breath and glared.

Laine shook her head. "Uh, I'm not completely convinced that they should meet either. Braden hasn't even come over. What if this angers him, and it spurs conflict in their family?"

Jazmine buried her face in her hands. "I can't refuse her *her* grandson. I now know how that must hurt."

Zara sighed. "I can't make up my mind—whether I like it or not. Who told her anyway?"

"Braden?" Jazmine suggested.

"It can't be. He wouldn't have the balls to break something like this to his mother," Anne cut in. "It must've been Gabe."

Jazmine gasped. "Gabe doesn't know anything about this."

"You don't think so?" Anne challenged.

Jazmine's shoulders slumped, and she shrugged. "What does it matter? Tita's coming next week."

"Is she coming with Braden?" Anne growled. "Do you want us to be here?"

Jazmine shook her head. "She said it would only be her."

Fiona had always welcomed Jazmine to family dinners and get-togethers, made sure that Jazmine had tasted every dish on the table, and urged her to join them in out-of-town trips. Jazmine had tried to accept most of the older woman's invitations, even though she sometimes felt out of place in their celebrations. Their family surely had more to spend than hers ever did. But being the girlfriend of Fiona's only child, Jazmine was always received with open arms.

Now, I wonder how she would feel about me . . .

The next day early in the afternoon, Anne called Zara. "Are you free now?"

"Yes, I'm just snacking on *lechon paksiw*.[11] What's up?"

Anne snorted at this.

"What, it's yummy! You were the one having food orgasms last night."

"I had to work out this morning just to get all the fat off me. Is Laine there?"

"No, she flew to Bohol this morning."

Zara and Laine rented an apartment together at the Le Sure Condominium in Makati City.

"How long will she be there?"

"She'll be there for the weekend only. What's up?"

"Be ready in ten minutes. I'll come pick you up at your condo."

---

[11] A Filipino pork dish made from leftover lechon cooked in vinegar and garlic

Anne hung up. Zara stared at the mobile and shook her head.

In ten minutes, Anne drove by the condo, and Zara stepped into her car.

"Anne, what's going on?" she asked as she buckled herself in.

"We're going to go check on Braden and see what he's been up to. I've got nagging doubts about Tita helping Jaz out."

Zara sighed. "Anne, you know that that is none of our business, right? Although I also meddle, I don't want Braden to be around Jaz anymore."

"Well, let's just check him out. I want to know if this guy who's been with Jaz for two years . . . two years . . . if he's now changed his mind, might be coerced by his mommy dearest to answer for Liam, or . . . if he'll continue to stay away from our little boy."

Zara sighed but resigned herself to her fate for the afternoon as Anne pulled out of the driveway and onto the highway.

As they neared the apartment that Braden was renting in Quezon City, Anne turned the car to park at the opposite side of the road.

"By the way, I messaged Jake last night and told him he was a douche." Anne winked at Zara.

Anne and Zara had some classes in college together, which was how they met. Anne had met Jake then while mingling in several social circles.

"Thanks?" Zara chuckled and shook her head at her friend. "So why do you care so much about Braden? Are you going to stalk Jake sometime soon too?"

"Well, among all of us, I've always disliked him the most. And he hit on me once while he and Jaz were still together. I want to destroy him in her eyes. If you must know, deep inside, Jaz still wants to get back with Braden."

They were not sure if Braden was home or if he was even in the city this weekend. Anne searched Braden's Facebook page for any clues. No posts since a week ago. And even then . . . a video of a dog doing tricks. A clip of a rock band concert.

Anne then plucked a pair of binoculars from the glove compartment.

Zara raised an eyebrow. "Why do you have binoculars?"

Anne waved a hand at Zara and brought the binoculars to her eyes. Anne trained them on the windows of Braden's apartment.

"Races."

Zara rolled her eyes.

"I can't see!" Anne blurted out and leaned forward in her seat. "I think someone's watching TV, but I can only see the back of his head. The windows are sort of tinted."

"Is it Braden?" Zara reached for the lenses but was shooed away.

"I can't tell. Although, who else would it be?" Anne raised her hands up in the air. "It's okay. We're not in a rush. Let's relax for a while."

Anne turned on the stereo in the car, and they chitchatted about the latest movies and sitcoms. After an hour, they saw Braden step out of the apartment and go to the barbecue vendor a block away. The barbecue vendor had a cart parked on the sidewalk, where he grilled chicken wings and pork cutlets.

"Yes, he's here!" Anne pumped her fist in the air. "I wish he'd do something stupid. Like trip on himself."

Anne and Zara turned in their seats to peer at him, resisting the urge to go and get some barbecue for themselves as well. After making his purchase, Braden went back to his apartment with a paper bag tucked under his arm.

"Nothing happening here, Anne. Maybe we should just let him be." Zara settled back in her seat and sighed.

"The shit is buying chicken barbecue while his son is crying back home and keeping his mom sleepless."

"If we really wanted to find out if he's talked to Tita Fiona about Liam, we should tap his phone," Zara suggested.

Anne frowned. "Do we know anybody who can do that?"

Zara shook her head. "Unfortunately none that I know of."

Anne's eyes narrowed at the apartment in front of them. "Just one more hour."

Half an hour later, they saw Braden walk out of his apartment with a woman clad in a light blue flowing dress. They were not touching each other. However, by the way she looked at him over her shoulder—her body twisted at an angle that emphasized her tiny waist, her chin dipped to suggest a shyness—before opening the door of the car parked outside his apartment, Anne and Zara could tell they had chanced upon something. Zara quickly snapped a photo of the twosome before the girl climbed into the car.

"Do you think Jazmine knows her?" Anne breathed.

"I can't tell. They've broken up for some months now. I'm not surprised that he's dating again, but it looks like he's already intimate with whoever she is . . . Do you want to tell Jaz?"

Zara braced herself for Anne's decision. Anne breathed in deeply.

"I can't." Anne sighed in disappointment with herself. "But if the time comes, just be ready with that picture. It might convince Jaz to drop the Palmas altogether."

CHAPTER SIX
Laine and the High-Rise

Laine settled her *sarong* on the rocky ground under a tree and sat on it. She could feel the rock's edges jutting out under her; nevertheless, she put on her sunglasses and earphones, leaned back, and surveyed the area and the sea beyond the short cliff.

It was the last property her father acquired before he passed away—an undeveloped property on Panglao Island, off the beaten track. Laine went there when she wanted some time alone. Her father was a religious man and was a minister at the local church. He used to tell her how everybody needed quiet time. Even Jesus.

She had gone home for the weekend to visit her mother and just escaped the relatives offering her all sorts of local dishes, bickering on whose cooking most delighted the girl who came home from Manila. She had feasted on her mother's *halang-halang*[12] and *buwad*[13] for breakfast, which had always been her favorites, and knew any more would be overkill.

She prayed, thinking about her father, her mother, and her friends in Manila. She still worried about Zara, who walked around their condo unit with a glassy look in her eyes. Jazmine

---

[12] A Visayan dish cooked with chicken or pork and is stewed in coconut milk and chili

[13] Dried fish or squid, which can be pungent, with a crunchy and chewy texture

had gotten thinner than she was before her pregnancy, but she told Laine she was happy she was losing the weight.

Laine tied up her hair in a ponytail, took off her shorts, and looked around. In all the times that she had been in that place, there had never been another soul. Then again, it never hurt to check. She took off her razorback tee and adjusted her bikini. She usually covered up herself more, but here she wore the one bikini she had for sunbathing.

She went down the stone steps with her snorkel and fins and dog-paddled her way through the water. Her father had taught her how to swim when she was a child, and since then, she and the sea had begun a love affair. Her tanned skin and well-toned body were proof enough.

She skin-dived a few times to the bottom of the sea to check if new corals had grown since she last came home. After a while she became satisfied that the older corals were as healthy as before.

When she surfaced for air, a voice called out from the cliff, "Oi!"

Laine turned to see who had trespassed on her personal retreat. There was a man standing on her father's property, waving at her. She swam closer to shore, ready to tell the man off.

"Excuse me. This is private property."

"Laine?" the guy asked, peering at her as she treaded in the water.

She strained to see his face, but the sun glared, and she squinted. She stepped out of the water and climbed up the steps, covering her body with her arms. She put on her tank top and approached the guy. He looked like he was about her age; he was wearing a tank and board shorts just like her.

"Yes?" She stood in front of him and had to look up.

"Your mother told me I'd find you here." He crossed his arms, and his eyes danced as he took in her confusion.

"My mom? Who are you?"

"You don't remember me at all?" He chuckled.

"I'm sorry. I really don't."

Laine's eyes suddenly roamed over the built arms, which pressed against his muscular chest, which led to his slim waist, which . . .

Snap out of it!

She hugged her waist.

"It's me, Antonio."

She gasped. "Tony! Is that you?" She gaped at him, suddenly recognizing the matured features of her childhood neighbor.

"Yes!" Without any warning, he hugged her and gave her a kiss on a cheek.

Before she could conceal it, Laine drew a sharp breath. Her cheeks burned up, and she could only hope her tan covered it up. He studied her, his arms still lingering around her waist. Realizing he must have crossed a line, he moved away, laughing.

"Sorry, too forward a hello?"

She chuckled but could not find the words to put him at ease or apologize.

"When did you come back? It's been ages." She giggled. "You talk differently too."

He and his mother, Evelyn, came back from the United States to Bohol a week ago. When relatives and friends heard, they had been invited for *merienda*,[14] lunch, and dinner in many homes. They visited Laine's mother the other day. Laine was

---

[14] A light meal usually taken for brunch or in the afternoon, filling in the gap between breakfast and lunch or lunch and dinner

surprised that her mother did not mention this.

"I see you're still the little mermaid you were. You look tanner now."

"Yes, I am! But I'm not so little anymore. Do you still swim?"

"I'm sure I can still beat you in a race," he teased. Back in the days, among the neighborhood kids, he was the one who could run the fastest, do backflips, and climb the tallest trees.

"Are you sure? I think the humidity and heat over here might be too much for your Am-boy lungs." She smiled. "I can't believe I didn't recognize you." She shook her head.

"Where are you these days?" he asked.

Laine sat on the lone wooden picnic table in the lot. She started toweling her hair and body dry.

"I work in Manila, so I only fly back here every three months or so."

"Fancy. Uh . . . I have a business. I run an online shop in the U.S."

"You mean like eBay?"

"It's more like Amazon, but I only sell sporting gear, particularly for cycling, sports wear, that kind of thing. It's still pretty localized, but people like that because they can just drop by our warehouse."

"Wow, that's impressive. You miss this place?"

"Very much. I miss the heat. I hate winters."

Suddenly a pickup truck drove into the small road beside the property. After the vehicle parked, Laine's mother and Evelyn stepped out, each one carrying a food hamper.

Laine smiled when she saw the older woman and ran to her. "Tita!"

Evelyn smiled and offered her hand. Laine brought it to her forehead, receiving her blessing.

"How are you, Tita? I can't believe Mom didn't tell me you were here." Laine peered at Vivian, who in turn smiled mischievously.

When they became friends in the local high school, Vivian and Evelyn had been inseparable. Even after they settled down and had children, they set up homes in the same neighborhood. However, they had to part ways when Tony's father received a job offer in Virginia. Two years after they moved, Pablo left his family for an American woman. Vivian had begged Evelyn to come back to the Philippines, but Evelyn did not want to uproot Tony once again.

"Well, Tony here wanted to surprise everybody," Evelyn shared.

Laine grinned. Tony had always been into pranks and surprises.

"Why did you bring a lot of food? Are we having lunch here?" Laine asked.

"You've slimmed down a lot. Manila is working you to the bones. And Evelyn brought some fresh seafood," Vivian answered.

Laine gasped. In Manila, she would have to go to Dampa, which was far from the condo, for a seafood feast at a decent price.

"Let me help with that! Can we eat now? I sooo miss prawns and crabs."

Her hands moved, opening containers and laying out plates. They settled down to eat. Laine groaned in appreciation every time she put a piece of seafood into her mouth.

"What are you staring at, fair-skinned man?" she teased when Tony laughed at her.

"Nothing." He choked and coughed. "I'll be sure to get under the sun more while I'm here."

"Laine, you know, Tony has opened his online shop in Virginia, and it's doing quite well." Evelyn smiled. "Maybe you should come and visit us sometime. We can take you around, see the Washington Monument . . ."

"He did tell me, and that's impressive. It'd probably take me some time to save up for a trip to the U.S. though."

Vivian grinned. "I'd be willing to help out."

"Me too," Evelyn put in much too quickly.

Laine stared at them. Tony shook his head and chuckled under his breath.

"Are you two trying to—"

"Don't say it. It'll drive them further on," Tony interrupted her. Their mothers' faces fell, but then he quipped, "But yeah, you should visit. Spring or autumn should be lovely. Some cherry blossoms here and there." He cleared his throat though there was nothing caught in it.

Laine stared at the two mothers. "I would, but it's just much too expensive for me. I got a few trips lined up, but they're all only domestic." Looking at Tony, she asked, "When are you going back? Maybe you could join me and my friends on our trips before you leave the country."

"Just friends. No boyfriend," Vivian interjected.

"Mom!" Laine grumbled and looked down at her plate.

Of all the times . . . And of all the things to say . . .

"Really? No boyfriend. You're too"—throat clearing—"beautiful to still be single."

Laine's mouth hung open—they were with both their mothers. "Well, I-I haven't been rushing or anything. Just busy with work and projects."

There was silence for a while as both mothers clutched each other's hand under the table.

"Tony doesn't have a girlfriend either," Evelyn ventured.

45

"Darn, Mom," Tony groaned at his mother. "*This* is why I had to get my own place."

The two mothers laughed, and Laine could not help but laugh along.

After lunch, they packed the food. Vivian and Evelyn planned to go back to the city.

Tony faced Laine. "Thought maybe we could drive around the city and the island?"

Laine hesitated and was about to look at her mom, when Vivian offered, "You kids go and enjoy your vacations."

Tony grinned in relief. "I'll bring her back home, Tita."

Tony pulled out of the subdivision and drove in the direction of the main road.

"I'm sorry to hear about your dad," he muttered under his breath.

"That's fine. He was sick for a long time . . . It was painful to let him go, but it was a relief for him." Laine stared out the window for a while. It had been three years since her father passed away from leukemia. "Mom's doing quite well. She won't take in a helper though, so I make sure to come home every now and then."

"He was like an uncle to me. Though I barely kept in touch over the years. Sorry about that too."

He laid his hand on hers. She squeezed it and smiled at him.

Wanting to lighten the mood, she asked, "How did you start your business?"

"I studied business admin at a university. The family of my classmate Ben was running a sports shop—they already had five branches. They hired me as part of operations management—I was pretty lucky." He chuckled and glanced at

Laine. "Anyway, I threw the idea of starting an online shop at Ben, who loved it. We became partners, hired a group of IT-savvy guys to make the online site, and now we're doing quite well . . . We've gone to five cities in the state already." He tried to stop it, but a smirk crossed his face.

"Wow, that's really gutsy."

"I wanted Mom to stop working as soon as possible. I was not an easy child to deal with, especially for a single mom."

"Oh, why don't I believe that," Laine quipped.

He laughed. "But . . . she still works part-time now because she gets bored just sitting at home. At least she makes friends at work and chitchats."

"That's nice. Mom still does her insurance gig. I don't give her a lot, but she gets some pension because of Dad."

"So you got no plans to leave the country and try something new?"

Laine shook her head and smiled. "I love my life here. I can go home to Mom. I enjoy my job, and I got the best girlfriends in Manila."

He nodded his head as if to accept that, but then he regaled her with accounts of spring and fall, interstate road trips, underground caverns, and the Capitol Hill. Laine got lost in the conversation as his face lit up over the stories he told.

"What do you say, let's go to Loay? Jump off the waterfall like we used to when we were kids." He grinned at her.

"Oh no. I never jumped before, and I still wouldn't dare. Heights scare me." She shook her head vigorously. "I'll go with you but only to watch."

"Yes! Here we go."

Tony and Laine slowly walked up the rocky slope that led to the top of the cliff. Every time the slope got steeper, he offered his hand out to her. At the top, the ground was covered with moss because of the cool temperature and looked slippery. Laine stayed far away from the edge while admiring the gushing waterfall across them.

"I just realized that if you jump into the water, I'd have to walk by myself all the way down. Didn't think this through." She gritted her teeth as she saw how far the waterfall was jutting down.

"Then you're going to have to jump with me." He started toward her with a smirk on his face.

"No, no. I'm not going with you. I'm—"

"What? The little mermaid is scared of the water?"

"It's not the water I'm scared of. It's the falling part." She shook her head when he moved toward her. "Oh no, no. None of those pulling other people down with you, like when we were kids."

Her eyes widened when he pulled her close to his chest. He tucked the hair that fell on her face behind her ears and tugged gently at her ponytail. Her eyebrows were drawn together, her lips stretched, and she struggled to break his hold.

"Tony, don't you dare. We're not kids anymore."

"Yes, we definitely aren't kids anymore." He grinned at her. "Before the hour is over, you'll be jumping down there yourself."

"O-okay. Good luck with that then." Her voice shook as she took in how close they were to each other.

Suddenly, his face softened, and his hold loosened. "Your eyes . . . they . . ."

Before she could think of getting away or what he was talking about, he laid his lips on hers. She froze. When he continued to kiss her lips over and over again, she relaxed and held on to his chest. He stopped, then smiled at her heavy-lidded eyes.

"Did y-you like that?" he asked, breathing unsteadily.

She trembled. It was the first time someone had kissed her that way. "Y-yes."

He stared at her for a while, brushing a finger along her jawline. Then he leaned down toward her ear and whispered, "Imagine that you're by a beautiful wall reef. Budding, colorful. You've spotted a shoal of silver jacks ten meters below."

Her breath caught in her throat when his breath brushed against her neck.

"Are you imagining them?" He looked at her face.

She studied his eyes.

Dark brown. Beautiful.

"Yes. Yes, I am."

"Imagine ten meters farther down." He held her by the hands. "Would you go? Would you dive deeper?"

Laine nodded. "I would."

"Imagine I'm holding you. I'm right beside you, and I'm not letting you go." He squeezed her hands. "Would you dive with me now?"

"Y-yes," Laine stuttered.

"Then close your eyes."

Laine's head snapped up at him.

"Hold your breath once you reach the water. I won't let go."

He pulled her closer and tightened his grip on her waist. There was no turning back now. She hugged his chest and wrapped her legs around him with viselike strength. She kept her eyes and mouth shut as she felt them both fall down the cliff.

After a beat, they splashed into the water. She felt the two of them plunge down the cold depth. She let go and swam up.

Before she knew it, her head bobbed up and down the surface of the water. Tony whooped, splashing the water and grinning from ear to ear.

Her heart hammered against her chest, and she floated on her back to calm down. She marveled at the waterfall cascading down, the birds flying around the cliff, the fresh air. Only a few other tourists were around.

"Laine . . ." He peered at her.

She closed her eyes and hummed, ignoring him. Her nostrils flared, her fists were clenched, but her heart was racing to a different beat.

Suddenly, he hauled her out of the water, hoisted her over his shoulder, and waded to the shore. Her eyes burst open, and she yelled at him.

"Put me down! You . . . you just made me do one of the scariest things ever!"

When they reached the shore, he put her feet back on the ground. He cupped her face; his hand crept up the back of her neck, trembling as it went. He kissed her.

She closed her eyes as everything around her became hazy. She let him take the lead, kissing back when she felt it must be right. Her heart beat wildly; she could not catch her breath. When she splayed her hands across his chest, she felt his heart beating just as madly. When her legs wobbled and she hung on to him, he broke the kiss and rested his forehead on hers.

"How can you still make me feel like this? After all these years."

"What?"

"Let's go home. It's getting dark, and your mother might get worried."

He pulled her to his side and slid his arm around her shoulders. They walked back to the car and dried up.

She did not speak as they drove back to the city. Every time he asked her to talk to him, she shook her head, waving his question away. Her heart had not slowed down, her body burned, and her cheeks flushed. Something in her belly, she could not comprehend it, stirred. She could not put a finger on it nor a lid, but she knew it was due to him.

Suddenly her stomach grumbled, and her garbled thoughts went away.

Tony scolded himself. "I'll text Tita and tell her we'll eat out before going home."

They stopped at an outdoor barbecue just outside the city. When they sat down opposite each other to wait for their order, Laine scanned the menu. Tony picked her hand up.

"Laine, I'm sorry. I thought it'd be fun to jump down the waterfall together."

"It was," she managed to blurt out but still avoided his gaze.

"Then why aren't you talking to me?"

She took her time answering. "You kissed me, and I don't know what to think about it."

She hummed and stared out at the open sky.

Take another leap, Laine. Take it with this man.

She shook her head.

No, he's not like the sea, not like an adventure. He's a mystery.

"You didn't like it," he suggested.

She shook her head.

"Was I being brash?"

She assessed that for a while and decided that Anne's and Zara's past boyfriends were more forward on occasion than Tony had been.

"I've never been kissed that way before."

With his suspicions confirmed, his lips broke out in a smile. "Did you like it?"

She was all nerves now and felt like such a prude.

It was just a kiss!

She peered at him and nodded honestly. Tony's smile widened, but his hand trembled. He stood up and slid next to her on the bench. He pulled her closer and lifted her chin up to him.

"I won't press for more than that."

He kissed her again. Laine felt her cheeks burn as she *tried* to kiss him back. She imagined people at the eatery staring at them as they would at any provincial setting. She hoped they would just think they were tourists passing through their beautiful town.

The next morning, Tony escorted Laine to church. Vivian always went to the early dawn mass on Sundays. Laine usually never woke up as early and often went to church by herself when in Bohol. When she found out that Tony was picking her up, she changed out of the black wrap dress she wore and put on a purple beach dress decorated with white and red swirls. When they arrived at the mass hall, Tony took her hand and led her to sit at the front pews.

At noon, Evelyn joined them at Laine's house for lunch.

"Tony, my *kumare*[15] Nadia called me," Evelyn started. "She complained that she saw you at church today wearing shorts. You should know better. We're not in the U.S., you know." Evelyn shook her head as she stirred her glass of iced tea. "She gave me a long talk about modesty inside the church."

Tony's mouth hung open. "What? I always wear shorts at church, and I've never been criticized before."

Laine snorted and gave him an I-told-you-so look.

---

[15] A close female friend who is the godmother of one's child or the mother of one's godchild

"This is the Philippines. It's a very close-knit community here. Everybody knows everybody. And . . . she complained that you were all over Laine at church."

She raised her eyebrows at her son while watching Laine from the side of her eyes. Laine's ears turned beet red. She suddenly became very intrigued by the pitcher on the table. She inched the pitcher in front of her so that Vivian and Evelyn could not see her face.

Tony's jaw dropped. "All over Laine? I didn't realize having my arm around her shoulders is considered being all over her. I was being very respectful."

Seeing Laine's state of red, Evelyn smiled and conceded.

Vivian chirped in, "Maybe she was jealous he didn't have his arms around Mara."

Laine choked and gave a small squeal behind the pitcher. Tony began to laugh at her, and she swatted him.

"This is the most awkward lunch," she grumbled.

Early the next morning, Tony took Laine to the airport for her flight back to Manila.

"Enjoy the rest of your stay here." She smiled up at him as she was about to enter the departure area.

She had learned from Anne that for some men, sometimes a kiss was just a kiss. Tony had not volunteered to keep in touch; he did not say he would. She assumed it was just a summer flirtation for him.

He wiggled his mobile in front of her and said, "Got your number. Have a safe trip, okay?"

She nodded and walked away. Romantically, this had been her best vacation, but now she just might have to forget him.

CHAPTER SEVEN

Jazmine and the Intersection

Jazmine primped Liam up as much as she could. She put on him a blue-collared shirt with a light blue whale-print bib and the khaki pants she bought the other day just for Fiona's visit. She set up his bouncer on the table by the couch so that she could place Liam there while she and Fiona talked.

Early that morning, Jazmine had stood by Liam's crib for fifteen minutes, watching him and wondering if she was doing the right thing by letting Fiona come into his life.

"I love you, baby. Even though Daddy isn't around, Mommy loves you just as much as two parents do together, okay?" she whispered to him. "And Mommy will work hard to give you everything two parents can give, okay? So don't worry about a thing. Mommy will take care of you."

She could still cancel the visit if she wanted to. But the best and worst scenarios running through her mind made her tired. She would give the relationship a try. She could change her mind later.

The bell rang. Jazmine took a deep breath and opened the door. Fiona stood there, donning a cropped do and dressed in a white sleeveless blouse with a lace yoke, cream tailored trousers, and nude pumps. Her face was made up—wine-colored lipstick, taupe eyeshadow, and eyeliner—and a pair of pearl earrings adorned her ears. Meanwhile, her slender hands clutched a branded mocha leather handbag.

Jazmine gulped. She had only the last of her clean nursing tops, an unfussy teal pull-down short-sleeve shirt, and stretchy shorts to wear that afternoon.

"Hi, Tita," Jazmine greeted. She winced when her voice squeaked. Her hand brushed over her hair and down her ponytail, tidying loose strands and tucking hair behind her ears. "Please come in."

"Hi, Jazmine." Fiona's slim lips smiled, and she leaned forward.

We're going to beso?[16]

Jazmine held her breath as their cheeks collided, once on her right cheek and again on her left.

This is so awkward.

Jazmine led the older woman into the apartment. Fiona's heels tapped on the floor as she entered.

I hope she doesn't mind my apartment. Her first time here, and it must smell like milk and spit-up. And possibly baby poop. Maybe her citrusy perfume will camouflage any odors there might be.

Fiona looked around the living room, pausing as her gaze landed on the sheer beige cotton curtains and, again, on the faux-leather couch set. When her eyes landed on the baby in the middle of the living room, she took a deep breath.

"Is that . . ."

"This is Liam." Jazmine gestured with a wave of her hand.

Fiona walked to the bouncer, reached in, and gingerly touched Liam by the sides. Liam stared up at her and then returned to fiddling with his plush owl hang toy.

Is she crying? Oh God, she's tearing up.

Fiona looked up at Jazmine and in a low tone breathed, "He

---

[16] Cheek-to-cheek kiss

looks just like Braden when he was a baby."

Jazmine stiffened, and she forgot to take a breath.

No. No, he doesn't. He's mine.

Calm down. She's here to help.

"I'm sorry." Fiona frowned. Her lips thinned. "I probably shouldn't have said that."

Jazmine merely nodded and then watched as Fiona talked to Liam, smiling and cheering him on to wrap his hand around her manicured pinkie finger.

He's mine. And yet my mother hasn't even seen him.

"Jazmine, you must be hard-pressed taking care of him," Fiona spoke, dashing Jazmine's hopes of an afternoon filled with only play and baby talk.

Yes, because your son refuses to help me.

The two women, now sitting on the couch, watched as Liam played with the toys on his bouncer. Fiona had taken off her watch and stored it in her handbag when Liam had become entranced by it.

The older woman laid a hand on Jazmine's arm. "I can help you."

Jazmine tensed at her touch and refused to look at her.

That would be nice. But what would that really mean for Liam? What would that mean for Liam and his father? His father and me?

When Jazmine did not say anything, Fiona continued, "I can take care of him for a couple of days each week. He can stay with us at home. You can get a night's rest. I know how much work it takes to care for a baby. And you can't be doing this alone."

"I'm getting a daytime nanny once I start working." Jazmine closed her eyes for a second and shook her head. "H-how would that work though? All his things are here."

"We can get stuff for him at home." Fiona gestured with her hands nonchalantly. "Let me know what stuff he'd need, which diapers and milk he takes . . ."

"He's being breastfed," Jazmine declared.

Fiona blinked and pursed her lips. "Of course. So . . . do you pump milk? Can you give me a batch each time you drop him off?"

Jazmine sighed and clasped her hands together. "Tita, does Braden know you're doing this?"

Fiona looked down at her wrist. "I've thrown the idea at him. Somehow he maintains—h-he doesn't want to get involved."

Oh my God. He really refuses to claim him. Even now.

Jazmine swallowed. Her hands shook, and so she gripped them more tightly together. She did not want Fiona to see.

It's just been me and Liam these past days. And the girls. I don't know if I can welcome another mother figure in Liam's life. A grandmother figure. Who isn't my mother . . .

Fiona continued to assure her. At the Palma residence, Fiona had household help who could support her around the clock. For the days that Liam was with Fiona, she would provide for his diapers and wipes, reducing Jazmine's expenses. Fiona would buy him bottles, a sterilizer, and a crib. She was sure Braden's father, Dennis, would agree to the arrangement.

"My son might not see it this way, but . . . we are family, Jazmine." Fiona took Jazmine's hands into her own. "And families stick together."

Jazmine looked into her eyes. She wanted so much to believe her.

CHAPTER EIGHT
Zara and the Pit

Zara made her way through the throng of people on the underpass escalator. When she got to the top, she walked to the white building around the corner.

The Makati streets were still awash with light and action. The metropolitan buildings were still lit; some professionals still worked, trying to rake in more money. Masses of cars waited for their turn to drive through the intersection between Ayala Avenue and Paseo de Roxas. Public buses and *jeepneys* honked to draw passengers on the streets. People rushed about their way down the underpass or to the loading stops.

At the second story of the building, Zara entered the Japanese modern-Zen restaurant Sushi Kyu. It was a posh enough place that Zara knew she could have dinner by herself without anybody walking up to her and being a bother. This night, the place was perfect, because she needed to unthink.

Delicious food, a couple of drinks . . . that should fix me . . . for tonight.

A staff in a pink kimono greeted her at the reception and led her to a corner table. She looked around. Men and women in stuffy business suits dined on granite countertop tables. She took a deep breath and relaxed.

"Is it only you, ma'am?" the lady asked.

"Yes." A snap was at the tip of her tongue, but she bit it

back.

Yes, I'm alone, dammit.

Sensing her irritation, the lady took the extra placemats and cutlery, bowed, and left her to peruse the menu. In a few minutes, a waitress came with a pot of tea.

"Salmon teriyaki and nama genshu sake please," Zara gave her order to the waitress, waving the tea away.

She relished the dinner, taking her time with the sashimi that came with the set. The first bottle of sake addled her.

Suddenly, the thought of waking up in Cebu after Jake had left jolted her to attention. She shook her head as if that would remove the mental picture from her thoughts, but the image of the empty room save for her and her luggage gripped her.

No . . . Shit. I need another drink.

"One more sake please," she asked the waitress, motioning to her sake bottle. The waitress nodded and bowed to her in response before going back to the bar to get her drink.

During the past two weeks, she had replayed the events of that weekend in her mind over and over again. Their reunion, the fun, the sex, the fight, and then the end. What he said, what she said . . . She did not want to feel but wanted to know at which moment things could have turned around. She did not want to react but just wanted to recall his expressions, his gestures.

Jake giving up after she gave him her ultimatum had been the hardest to swallow. She knew it had been coming, that the breakup was for the best, but she had hoped he would have turned things around.

He might've been waiting for me to do it . . . the breakup . . . Shit! God, when will I stop thinking about this?

Her second sake arrived, and she gulped it down. *Whoa! Numb, not dumb.*

She needed to walk out the restaurant by herself and at least get a taxi.

After finishing dessert and a fourth sake, Zara opted to walk back to her condo on the other side of Ayala Avenue, which was five blocks away. Late in the night, when the streets were empty and people were not fighting their way into public utility vehicles, the streets of Makati could pass for wistful.

As she walked along Paseo de Roxas leisurely, silently cursing the dark sky and the romantic lights from buildings and street posts, her mobile rang. She stopped in her tracks and reached into her handbag.

"Please let it be someone who wants to go out for a drink. Darn!" She frowned when she saw the caller appear as "Unknown."

She hesitated; she had received a couple of calls from telemarketers that week. She answered the call and swaggered forward. "Hello?"

"Zara, where are you? I can hear cars." Jake. His voice was the familiar baritone that used to speak to her every night before she went to bed. Well, almost every night.

She stopped in her tracks again, and her body stiffened.

Why does he have to call now?

"I'm out," she blurted out.

"Who are you with?"

"Myself."

There was a pause. "Have you been drinking? Your voice sounds funny . . . How are you getting home?"

"I'm walking."

A sigh. "Can you send me a text message when you get home then?"

"No, I'll be too drunk by then." She snorted.

"What time do you think you'll be home?"

Zara hung up the phone. She stared at it for a while before it rang again. She answered the call.

"What did you do that for?" he demanded.

"Stop it! Stop acting like I answer to you."

"I just wanted to make sure you're all right." His voice softened.

"If that were true, you'd have called me the evening after you left me at a goddamn island that was three hours away from the goddamn city." She choked up and began to sob.

She walked to a nearby lamppost and leaned on it for support. A couple passing by glanced at her.

"Zara, I'm sorry. It was difficult for me to stay . . . You've always taken care of yourself. I thought you'd be fine then."

"I know you're accustomed to me looking after myself, but I'm also human, Jake. We just broke up then . . . Damn you." She sank down to the ground and sat on her ankles. "If you called just to find out if I'm okay, I'm okay, okay? If that's all, then stop calling me."

"I . . . I just thought . . . Okay. Goodbye, Zara. Take care."

She hung up on him before he could on her. She waited a while for the mobile to ring again, but it did not anymore.

She started walking toward the condo again. She muttered curses to herself for a minute and then breathed deeply, trying to calm herself down. She blinked again and again until she felt that the tears had all receded. Taking out her powder case, she primped her face up, trying to cover the red blotches on her skin. Laine knew she was broken, but Zara did not want to look like how she felt inside.

CHAPTER NINE

Jazmine and the Shoulder

Jazmine stepped into the bedroom of her apartment. She stared at the crib, where only a green stuffed dinosaur lay, and her insides clenched for the fifth time that day.

The first time her insides churned was when she brought Liam to the Palma residence at the San Antonio Village. It was just as she recalled: the white grill fence, the yard wide enough for a toddler to run around in, and the bisque country-style bungalow house. A grey Lexus was parked on two strips of cement surrounded by patches of green just at the back of the gate.

She was greeted by Sitti, the household help, who squealed in delight when she saw Liam. Jazmine refused to let her carry Liam though, saying that the baby just woke up from a nap and might cry. It was silly—Sitti would be helping Fiona in caring for him—but Jazmine wanted to hold her son until she had to leave. The maid told her to wait in the living room, and Jazmine turned her attention to Liam to settle her nerves. This room had always made her feel small.

A few minutes later, Dennis and Fiona came out of their bedroom and greeted the visitors. Jazmine sighed in relief when she did not seem out of place in jeans and a black tee, as the couple donned chino shorts and polo shirts. While his wife talked about the arrangements made for Liam's visit, Dennis would open his mouth once in a while as if to say something but would then close it.

The second time her stomach clenched was when Jazmine saw the pristine room that her son would sleep in. A wooden crib, with matching jungle-themed beddings and bumpers, was at one corner of the room. On the other side, on the floor lay a Parklon playmat and a Skip Hop play gym. An immaculate changing table, with a built-in organizer made of at least a dozen compartments, stood by the window. Fresh newborn clothes and towels were stacked up on the bottom shelves of a cabinet, while packs of diapers and wipes filled the upper racks. Jazmine swallowed. There was more in this bedroom than there had ever been in the home Jazmine had put together for Liam. Not even when she herself had first prepared for his birth.

The third time was when she left her son in the arms of his grandmother. At first, he kicked his little feet and squirmed, stretching his white booties. But when Fiona bounced him up and down and tickled him on the side, he let out a smile. He did not even cry for Jazmine. He was perfectly fine. And so *she* cried once she stepped out of the house's gate.

The fourth time was when she had gone to the office to meet with HR and make sure she had the proper documents for her medical claims. She was scheduled to go back to work in a week. She had pumped her milk in the copy room and then read the emails in her inbox, unopened for the last seven weeks, but her mind kept wandering to her son.

Is he okay? Are they attending to him? I told them he would cry every two hours for milk—will they listen for every sound that comes from his crib?

Jazmine had wanted to call Fiona right then but stopped herself.

She must know. She was a mother once too. Calm down. You're adjusting to being away from him, that's all. This is natural. This nagging feeling will go away sooner or later.

Now, in the early hours of the night, as she stood inside the empty bedroom of her apartment, all she could hear were the distant noises from the street outside and the faint croaks of a frog. And the heavy thoughts in her head.

C'mon! You can sleep peacefully tonight. Make the most of it. Liam is coming home tomorrow, and you'll be drowning in household chores again. You've got to catch up on the Unilab paperwork anyway.

She argued with herself over and over again, but all she really wanted to do was go to San Antonio and pick Liam up that very minute.

The next morning, Jazmine woke up with a start. Her eyes darted to the crib. The puny dinosaur still stared at the tan wall.

That crib looks smaller than it used to be.

She glanced at the wall clock.

Seven o'clock. Got to get to the office.

She was supposed to meet with Grace, her department manager, to discuss the plan on a joint project with Unilab.

There was a party at the office. It was the birthday of Michelle, one of the department's program facilitators whom Laine worked with.

Jazmine worked in the resource development of the health and nutrition segment of the Ganoop Children Foundation, while Laine handled education and youth empowerment.

I miss this. Being outside the house. Not having to be on my toes the entire time, waiting for somebody to cry.

After catching up with several other people, however, Jazmine found herself talking about Liam rather than asking people what had transpired in the office in the past seven weeks.

Suddenly Jazmine's mobile rang, and Zara's name appeared on the screen. Jazmine picked up, expecting the call. Zara had offered to drive her to the Palma residence to collect Liam that day.

"I'll be there at twelve," Zara announced. "I'll call you when I'm almost there."

"I should only be an hour more anyway. Thanks, Zara. I just . . . I just need the moral support this time . . . after seeing all the nice things Liam gets at their home . . ."

"Not a problem, Jaz. Is Laine coming with us?"

"Yeah, she said she will."

Zara hesitated. "Is Anne up for a lunch trip too?"

Jazmine sighed. "She called me up the other day and asked if I was going through with this. I said yes, and she scolded me again."

"Okay . . ."

"So I didn't ask her. She'll just keep discouraging me about this, Zara."

"You're right. It'll just be us then. Let's not fret. We're just fetching Liam. No biggie."

Zara parked the car outside the Palma house. The Toyota Corolla gave a little shudder as the engine died.

"Nice house. Not bad," Zara commented. "Quiet neighborhood."

Jazmine looked over her shoulders and scanned the area. Gated houses lined the street on both sides. Only a black Honda Civic and a grey Volvo were parked outside the neighboring houses—a different sight compared to the previous morning, when cars waited on the driveways for their turn to leave.

"This is the one, right, Jaz?" Laine asked, peering outside the window.

"Yes." Jazmine sighed. "Just checking if Braden's car is around."

Before the girls could berate her, Jazmine stepped out of the vehicle. She rang the buzzer. A few moments later, Sitti walked out of the house and opened the gate.

"Hi. I'm here to pick Liam up," Jazmine announced.

"Come in, Ate. We thought you'd arrive later." Sitti motioned her toward the door.

When Jazmine entered the house, Fiona just walked out of Liam's room. Jazmine blinked twice. Fiona wore a plain V-neck shirt and flannel shorts. And was without any makeup.

"Hi, Tita." Jazmine smiled and headed in her direction. "I'll be getting Liam now. Thank you so much for—"

"Hi, Jazmine." Fiona smiled and stepped in front of her. "Liam is still sleeping. Maybe you can get him a bit later?"

Jazmine's eyebrows furrowed.

"Oh, that's fine, Tita. I'll just pick him up and go," Jazmine insisted, making another move toward the room.

This time, Fiona held her by the arm and patted it. "They say it's not good to wake up a sleeping baby."

Jazmine regarded the hand on her elbow and inched her arm back.

"He'll be fine, Tita." Jazmine explained, "My friends are waiting for me in a car outside, and so I need to get him now."

Fiona glanced at Sitti, who was behind Jazmine.

Sitti said, "Yes, ma'am. There's a car waiting outside."

Jazmine frowned.

Why is she questioning what I just said?

Fiona smiled briefly at Jazmine. "Do you want to invite

66

your friends in? They can have some refreshments first."

Jazmine reined back a glare and instead shook her head. "Thank you, but I can't do that. My friends can't stay long. They need to go back to work."

Before Fiona could say anything more, Jazmine sidestepped her and went to the door. When she entered, she doubled back. Her son lay on a pale blue muslin crib sheet, while he wore a navy blue cotton onesie.

He looks peaceful . . . like in a Mothercare ad.

She shook her head, reached inside the crib, and lifted her son. He began to stir. She foresaw that a crying fit was about to come, and so she grabbed the diaper bag she had left behind with him.

Have they packed everything in this bag already? Oh, just leave already.

Her footsteps tapped on the diamond-patterned tiles of the hallway as she hurried out. When she passed by the living room, she spied Fiona sitting on the couch and staring at her hands. Jazmine stopped in her tracks. Right then, Liam woke up and whimpered.

"Tita, thank you for taking care of Liam," Jazmine acknowledged the other woman.

Fiona looked up and nodded. "Do you want to stay for lunch or merienda? Can you and Liam go home later?"

Jazmine shook her head and forced a chuckle. "I really can't. My friends are driving us home."

Fiona nodded yet again. "I-I'll see you again next week?"

"Yes," Jazmine agreed. "I'll let you know which day is good?"

Fiona held up a hand and put in, "Wait. I bought him a breathable pillow. And some new sheets. Maybe you should take those home with you." Fiona stood up.

"It's okay, Tita. Actually . . . he doesn't need a pillow just yet," Jazmine contended. "And he has bedsheets at home. Three sets should be enough."

The two women stared at each other for a while. Then Liam began to cry.

"Sure, of course." Fiona threw up her hands. "I recorded his feeding times—just as you requested. The notebook should be in that bag."

"Thank you." Jazmine smiled and waved. "Goodbye."

Fiona offered, "I can take care of him for three days if you need the break."

Without turning around, Jazmine replied, "I think two days is just fine, Tita. It's more than enough. Thank you again."

Once Jazmine got into the car, she opened the buttons of her shirt and let her son nurse.

"Did you get all his things?" Zara turned on the ignition.

Without paying heed to Zara's question and Laine, who shushed Liam, Jazmine held her son closer and showered kisses on his hair, forehead, and cheeks.

"Mommy's here. Mommy's here," she whispered into his ear.

Later that night, after putting Liam back to sleep, the three girls had dinner at Jazmine's apartment.

"Jaz, your creepy neighbor, Mr. Reyes, was looking at us when we walked in here tonight," Zara declared with a shudder.

"What? Oh, him? Don't mind him," Jazmine replied. "He's just weird—that's all."

"Still . . ." Zara shot a look at the direction of the other house.

"Did you get enough sleep last night?" Laine peered at

Jazmine.

"Yes." Jazmine blew out a breath. "I should pull an all-nighter tonight and play with Liam. Not a dull moment."

Zara and Laine looked at each other.

"Jaz, it's okay to rest," Laine started. "Everybody needs to rest."

"It's just that . . . I feel bad, having left him with somebody else—" Jazmine buried her face in her hands. "You're . . . you're right, of course. I'm being dramatic." She looked up. "I'm a little upset with Tita. I gave her instructions on how often Liam should be fed. But I see that she's fed him more than twenty-five ounces yesterday."

Laine laid a hand on Jazmine's. "Jaz, I know you're very particular about his milk. And nutrition and stuff. But now, you can't control everything."

"Try talking to Tita," Zara suggested. "It's their first two days with him. Maybe they panicked each time he cried?"

Jazmine nodded and stared down at her food. "Yeah, you're right. You're right."

When Jazmine stayed quiet, Laine placed her hand on top of Zara's.

"I should probably ask you if you've been having enough sleep too?" Laine grinned sheepishly at her.

Zara stiffened for a second but then covered Laine's hand with the other.

"Thanks. I'll come around soon enough. I'm still quite depressed. I just need to grieve, that's all." Zara started tearing up but shook her head and blinked back the tears.

Jazmine looked up and squeezed Zara on the arm. "We're here for you." Jazmine smiled at her. "Do you want to get some ice cream?"

Zara laughed, and a tear fell from her eyes. "No need for ice cream." She cleared her throat. "But . . . I'm not the one with the big news." She wiggled her eyebrows at Laine, but her smile did not reach her eyes.

Laine's mouth opened in shock.

Jazmine laughed. "I did get the feeling that something happened when you went home and a guy was mentioned."

"She hasn't told me the story yet, but she blushes every time she talks about it . . . and she refers to it as 'the weekend.'" Zara grinned while gesturing with air quotes.

"Laine, I never thought you'd have it in you," Jazmine kidded her friend.

Laine blushed. "We made out. Or that's what I think it is."

"Please elaborate."

"We kissed. He has the softest and . . . yummiest lips," Laine breathed dreamily. "I can't tell! It's just too private!"

They prodded her on until she gave in and told them what had happened with Tony.

Zara asked, "What's he up to now?"

"He texts me every day, but I'm not kidding myself. I still know too little about the grown-up Tony, and he lives all the way in the U.S."

"If he's as intense a guy as he sounds, I don't think that'll stop him," Jazmine mused.

"I don't mind if he doesn't make anything out of it. I'm actually scared about feeling this heady and attracted toward him. I don't feel like myself."

"You mean not like a Goody Two-Shoes?" Jazmine teased.

"Our Laine is growing up." Zara grinned.

Jazmine nodded at Zara and chuckled. "Amen to that."

CHAPTER TEN

Zara and the Big Ladder

Zara checked the desk across hers. The clock showed ten o'clock, but the desk was still empty. She frowned and checked her mobile if Gaea, her senior writer, had left any messages. They were supposed to turn in a main feature of the magazine to their manager by noon. Their editor in chief, Don, is known to raise his voice at delinquents whatever the size of the audience.

Zara had been working in the writing department of the travel magazine *Biyahe* for three years, but she had only been contributing bits and pieces of the content that Gaea asked for. Gaea controlled the composition and focus of the feature stories.

Suddenly, Don stepped out of his office and headed toward Zara's direction.

Uh-oh.

Zara sat up straighter, scanned her screen, and jotted a few notes in a pad, in hopes that Don would pass by without saying a word. He stopped right beside her desk and peered at her.

"Zara, can you step into my office?" he asked.

"Sure." She snatched her notebook and a pen, then followed him.

Don sat on the chair behind his desk and motioned for her to sit down.

"Gaea called me. She was in an accident last night. A man on a motorcycle tried to grab her bag as she was walking home." Zara gasped, and her hands flew to her mouth. Don shook his head. "Why she's walking on the goddamn streets so late . . . I don't know why. She fell. Got a bad sprain, gashes, and bruises . . . She had to go to the emergency room."

"Is she okay? Where did this happen?"

"She's traumatized, but she said she's recovering. Maybe you can check on her later. Then let me know if there's any improvement there." He paused, took a deep breath, and studied her for a moment. "She told me she'll send me the feature on Intramuros tonight. Actually, I wanted her to start on the next cover feature this week. Since she won't be physically able for another week . . ."

He continued, "I have some doubts . . . It'll be your first time to take the lead . . ." Suddenly his eyebrows furrowed at her. "You haven't even taken the advanced journalism course, have you?"

Zara opened her mouth to say that she was registered to take it the next month, but he held up a hand.

"I need you to write the article on the Hundred Islands." He clasped his hands in front of him and rested his chin there. "Consult with Ingrid on which of the photographers you can take with you. Can you do this?"

"Yes!" Zara almost shouted.

Don's lips thinned. "Good. I want a food article and a cultural perspective on the towns nearby." He leaned back in his seat. "Try out the *kaleskes*[17] and *pigar-pigar*.[18] Check with Leslie on the budget, will you?"

Her heart throbbed. "Sure. I'll do my best, Don. Thanks for

---

[17] A Pangasinense stew made up mostly of beef innards
[18] A Pangasinense dish made with strips of beef and stir-fried cabbage

this."

"I heard you got Gaea's assignment." Andrea, another writer, beamed at Zara.

Zara had just hung up the phone after talking to Ingrid, the art and design director.

"Yes! I feel bad about Gaea's accident, but I've been waiting for this for so long." Zara grinned at her. "It's the Hundred Islands."

"What's that again?" A voice behind Andrea made them cringe.

It was Matt, Andrea's senior writer and Gaea's office rival. He and Gaea always competed for the best places to report on and to write the cover, the mainstream feature, or the cultural feature. He stood up and narrowed his eyes at them.

"I pitched that idea to Don," he grumbled, ruffling his hair with his fingers.

Zara noticed this quirk of his. With the competition between him and Gaea, she had decided a long time ago that she did not like him.

"Well, I'm going to do my best with this assignment. I won't mess this up—," Zara started.

"Shoot. I had ideas for that cover already." His right hand went to his waist, and he pursed his lips.

"Care to share them with me?" Zara gave him her sweetest smile.

He stared at her for a while. "Sure . . . maybe." Then he sat down again.

After Zara called Gaea and made sure she was tucked in bed and drinking ginger ale, Zara pulled out every online article she could find on the Hundred Islands National Park—history,

73

geography, sites, and whatnot. She got in touch with the two photographers who were assigned to the feature, checked the budget for nonsponsored covers, and forecasted the expenses.

They would need a guide to take them around, somebody who knew the islands and the town. She phoned their contact in the Department of Tourism to ask about the accommodations, attractions, and tours. Their contact gave her five hotels and three local guides to check out. She found out that all of the hotels were midrange resorts with limited facilities.

After being on the phone for a couple of hours, she decided on getting Ramon, one of the guides recommended by the DOT and the most frequently mentioned by the hotel staff she spoke to. Deciding to book at the Alaminos Sunrise Resort, since the manager knew Don and was keen to appear in the magazine, she asked the hotel to get in touch with the guide and left her contact details. Ramon would need to pick them up at the resort on Thursday and take them out on a pump boat to island-hop.

She outlined her activities, making sure she would not miss a single thing. It was Tuesday. She would have to complete the paperwork for the trip the next day. Her team would have to leave Manila early Thursday morning.

She then called Laine. "Want to go to the Hundred Islands with me?"

"I want to! But when?"

"This Thursday." Zara heard pages being flipped from Laine's side and guessed she was checking her calendar.

"I think I can make it. Let me see if I can go on leave. This is for a feature, right? And we can laze around and swim?"

"Uh-huh." Zara reached for a postcard of a pink sand beach on the Sta. Cruz Island of Zamboanga that was on her cubicle wall. There were five other postcards beside it. "Get your swimsuit ready."

Anne and Jazmine could not make it for the weekend, so Zara had driven to Alaminos, which was the best takeoff point when touring the national park, with only Laine in tow. When they arrived at Alaminos, Zara spotted a black SUV parked outside the hotel they were going to stay in. Zara frowned and cursed. She hopped off her car and marched toward the SUV. She knocked on the driver's window.

"Matt, what are you doing here?" she asked as soon as the window was open. Matt smirked at her from inside the vehicle.

"Don asked me to assist you on your assignment."

"The hell," she muttered under her breath. "You're taking over? I've been really hoping for this break, you know. If I do well, Don might get me to do main features."

His grin grew.

The devil has the nerve to grin right now. Does he want me to beg or something?

"Well, I just thought, it's my pitch, so I should have some say." He shrugged and leaned an arm over the window frame.

She drew in a breath.

"I can take care of this," she insisted.

He burst out laughing and then shook his head. "I'm just messing with you. You should've seen your face just now."

When she heaved a sigh of relief, he continued, "Seriously though you need help on this because it's your first cover feature." He leaned his head toward the window and eyed her. "Do you have an angle you can work on?"

"Yes, I have lots," she snapped. She shook her head at herself. Trying for a softer tone, she said, "Sorry. I mean, I have lots."

He stared at her for a while. "Good."

Gaea seemed to get her angles only during the fieldwork, but

75

I've got plans A, B, and C. I should be able to pull this off, right?

"If you want to, y-you can go back to the city," she suggested.

Please go back.

"As much as I'd want to do that—it's almost weekend after all—Don asked me to at least get an angle of my own in case you don't come up with something solid." He raised his hands, indicating his innocence in the idea. "His words, not mine."

She seethed. "Did you tell him I won't be able to do this?"

I'd just have to do my best and let my work speak for itself.

"Of course not." He smirked. "I can't say he doesn't think that though."

Her jaw ticked. He was so sure of himself, but she knew it was for a good reason. He was Don's golden boy and knight in shining armor. He threw ideas at meetings that made management nod their heads, smile, and then concede. When Zara read his features for the magazine, she always felt a sharp curiosity for the places he described.

"You—"

"Excuse me," a voice beside her cut off her tirade. "Are you Zara?"

Her head snapped to her left. A man in his midforties approached her, and she knew she was going to have to put the battle on hold for Ramon.

"Mang[19] Ramon, what's that island over there?" Zara asked.

Since that morning, Zara, her team, Matt, and Laine had been on a boat, hopping from one island to another. The group had visited five islands earlier, about which Zara did not learn any more than what she already had through the Internet.

---

[19] A title for a male who is older, usually used as a sign of respect

Zara's team consisted of JT and Keith, the photographers, and Missy, the designer. She had worked with Missy and JT before and did not hesitate sharing her ideas with them and giving them directions. However, Keith was a senior photographer who just joined the magazine. He only grunted after being talked to and went about his own way on each island with his equipment. If Gaea were there, she might already have called him out on his aloofness, but Zara would not dare risk vexing him.

Ramon looked at where she was pointing and answered, "That's the Black Island. That's not part of our usual tour packages. There's a cave on the island, but people don't go there . . ." His eyebrows furrowed and he looked away. "Because of the bats."

"A cave on an island? What about the locals, do they go there?" She continued to stare, narrowing her eyes at the small island surrounded by white sand and made more prominent by the brooding cave flanked by trees.

"They prefer not to. There's a local legend about a man and a woman who pledged to leave Alaminos to be together—their families forbade their union. They planned to meet one night over there . . . at the Black Island, then sail to Dagupan to start a new life together. Too bad . . . there was a storm the night they were to escape. The woman got lost at sea, drowned. The man arrived at the island and waited. He waited for days until he couldn't deny it anymore—he had lost her to the sea. He grieved in the cave and eventually killed himself . . . That's why it's called the Black Island."

Mysteries and legends . . .

"Everything sounds so ominous . . . Let's go!" Zara grinned at the group.

When they reached the Black Island, Ramon led them

around the island. On their way back to the boat after the excursion, Zara had a huge grin plastered on her face, and her mind was working in overdrive. Black Island was just the angle she was going to use to make the feature intriguing. Matt saw the grin and immediately knew what she was thinking.

"This would've been my angle too." He patted her on the back and smiled at her. "I can share my thoughts with you if it'll help."

She regarded him for a while. "Thank you." Then she mumbled to herself, "As long as you promise not to sabotage this for me."

The next day after breakfast at the resort, the group went to the small port of Alaminos. Zara had arranged for parasailing. She hoped they could get some aerial shots of the islands. There was only one speedboat in town, and the parasail was for pairs. Keith and JT were sailing through the air as the speedboat glided through the water.

"Zara, I'm not going parasailing. You know I'm scared of heights," Laine insisted as Zara prodded her to join her on the parasail.

"Scared of heights?" Matt quipped.

Laine nodded. "I'm a scaredy-cat."

"A scaredy-cat who's gone night diving." Zara rolled her eyes. "Don't believe her. She's a certified advanced diver who cleans up our seas regularly."

"That's ironic, but I get it." Matt smiled at Laine with new regard. He turned to Zara. "You want company up there?"

Zara gawked at him.

I'm not really keen on going up there with you.

"I can hold your hair when you puke." His eyes egged her on.

Zara gave him a black look. "Fine, we can go together."

"Just so you know, Zara has gone parasailing a number of times on different islands." Laine stared Matt down.

He simply chuckled and shook his head.

"This is a nice view!" Zara yelled and turned to Matt.

From above, they could see the islands that they had visited the day before and the many limestone islets that earned the attraction its name. He chuckled and nodded in agreement. He took out his mobile to take pictures.

"Just let me know when I need to hold your hair." He turned to her and winked.

"Why do you tease me so? I know you're a senior in the department, and I'm just a junior staff . . . but still."

"You're not so junior, Zara. Otherwise, you wouldn't have gotten this gig. Don actually likes you, which is why he's taking this chance."

"Really?" She beamed at him.

He nodded as he continued taking pictures. "As for me, I'm just being sociable."

"Well, if that's what being sociable means . . . ," she grumbled and pursed her lips.

Matt laughed as he stared at her. "You're pretty cute when you're pouting."

Zara muffled the gasp that escaped her, but before she could say anything to Matt, he was back to taking pictures. She decided to dismiss his comment, but her mind acted on its own and busied itself by putting all sorts of meaning into what he said. She tried to shake the thoughts away.

That night, Zara and Laine went to check out the only bar in town. Missy decided to turn in early because she was tired.

Streetlamps flickered, but the girls walked leisurely along the dimly lit road outside their hotel. The moon shone, and the stars twinkled on the quaint town of Alaminos.

Kapitan's Bar was a rough and rowdy place with bamboo tables and chairs spread out in the open air. A group of tipsy old men sat by the table nearest the videoke. Judging from their homey wear, they were locals out for the night, just drinking Pale Pilsen and taking turns singing Tagalog love songs. One of them was singing Pedrito Montaire's "Be My Lady." Or slurring is more like it.

Matt, JT, and Keith were already there when Zara and Laine arrived. They were drinking beer and chatting. Even Keith was all smiles, his face already pinkish.

"Well, they're so chummy," Zara muttered. "Argh! He's got such tight connections at the office."

She zipped up her cotton jacket and hid her hands inside the sleeves as they made their way toward the matey trio.

"Why is that a bad thing? He seems to tease you fairly often." Laine grinned at her. "I can see you're reining back your irritation with some effort. You've never mentioned him to me before, and yet . . ."

"He's my boss's backup plan in case I screw this up," Zara grumbled. "So I hate him."

Laine cringed at this piece of information but then grinned.

"Do you hate him? Or do you think he's hot? I know your type, Zara, and he's pretty close," Laine teased.

Zara gasped. "Shut up."

She stole a glance at Matt. He was wearing a black long-sleeved sweater and board shorts. The wind blew at his short tousled shag. Every now and then, he reached up and brushed his hair back with his fingers. She gulped.

"Zara, if you like this guy, please don't sing here tonight."

Laine laughed.

Zara gawked at her. "First, you know I don't sing when there are people from the office. Second, I don't like him."

Zara only sings around her three best girlfriends and for good reason; every time she sang, and she always did with heart, her friends either cringed or laughed out loud. Tonight, she was just a writer, an observer to the local festivities.

CHAPTER ELEVEN

Jazmine and the Mommy Highway

He did not roar like an alpha lion whose reign was over. No, he wailed like a banshee.

Liam would not stop crying. No matter what song or sway Jazmine tried, he just would not stop. She tried breastfeeding him, but after nursing for a while and falling asleep, he would spit up, wake up again, and wail like she was the worst mother in the world. His crib sheets had been soiled by his spit-ups, but she never got the chance to change them.

Why do women in breastfeeding photos look so calm and peaceful? Those advertising campaigns are so misleading!

She prayed with her eyes clamped shut and her lips pursed that Liam would calm down already and go to sleep. It was four o'clock in the morning. Only a weak night-light glowed at one corner of the room. She had slept for only two hours before Liam woke her up.

Lord, please let him go to sleep!

She sang a nursery rhyme she had not tried that night, lightly bouncing her arms up and down as she held him close. Her arms ached, and she was out of breath. However, she had no choice but to try over and over again; there was only her, after all.

Lord, please let him go to sleep. Please let him go to sleep.

Slowly, Liam closed his eyes. His breathing deepened. Not

wanting to risk another crying episode, Jazmine waited for five more minutes before heading to the rocking chair with Liam still in her arms. Even as she moved, she continued to bounce him up and down and sing the same song over and over again. When she sat down, she held her breath.

Would he feel the difference? Thank God he didn't wake up!

She dared not lay him down in his crib. She settled herself in the chair, putting as many pillows around her arms so that she would not drop him, and she drifted off to sleep herself.

Liam woke up again after a couple of hours.

Two more hours of sleep . . . Yeeeey . . .

With her arms aching from cradling him for hours, she managed to open the top buttons of her shirt and breastfeed him. Her head bobbed up and down as she struggled to keep awake.

"Jazmine, how are you and Liam?" Fiona smiled at the mother and son as Jazmine came to drop Liam off that morning.

"Tita, he kept me up all night last night. I'm so sleepy right now." Jazmine looked down at her son.

It was the third week that Jazmine dropped Liam off with Fiona. Jazmine had grown accustomed to the brown leather couch in the living room, the glass table in front of the television where Sitti would serve her iced tea, and the '50s abstract low-pile rug in the middle of the room. She had also come to know the creaks that came from the hallway—if the door opened led to Fiona's bedroom or Liam's.

Fiona smoothed a white muslin cloth over her shoulder and took Liam in her arms. "Oh dear. Do you have to work today?"

"Unfortunately I do. I think he's in a phase where he likes to sleep during the day and only a few hours in the night." Jazmine smiled and said, "I have to say that getting a few days of rest for the past weeks has been a big help."

"That's good to hear." Fiona beamed.

Jazmine's smile grew as Liam made himself comfortable against Fiona's chest. Fiona wore loose denim shorts and a plain white V-neck shirt. Her slim face, touched up with only a little powder, brightened when Liam burbled.

"How are things at work? How are the hours?" Fiona asked and motioned Jazmine to sit down on the couch.

Jazmine's mouth opened an inch.

She's never asked about just me.

"Uh, things are fine. Just that . . ." Jazmine smiled, recalling having lunch with Laine and Rhonda. "Most days, I need to rush home from the office." She hesitated, and when Fiona's head bobbed, Jazmine continued, "Uh, one time, I arrived an hour behind schedule. Ate Helen and the driver were nice about it, but I felt horrible. The driver went home to his family late that night because of me."

Fiona nodded and peered at Jazmine. "How's the pay at the foundation though? Is it worth the effort you're putting in?"

Jazmine sighed and studied a wet patch on her navy blue and ivory striped skirt. "I don't eat at fancy restaurants as often as my friends do . . . And I don't shop as much either. But I love my job. I belong in this field."

Fiona took a deep breath. "Braden did tell me about the work you do."

Jazmine grinned at Fiona, but the older woman merely shifted Liam closer to her shoulder. Jazmine frowned and scratched the blot on her skirt.

Fiona asked, "So . . . tell me about the neighborhood you're in. Just being curious, if you don't mind."

Jazmine chuckled and said she did not mind at all. She has rented the apartment since she joined Ganoop, loved having the place all to herself, and relished the times her family visited her there.

"Braden had mentioned to me once that you have quite a character for a neighbor," Fiona put in.

Jazmine curled her legs under her and chuckled. "A character? No. Mr. Reyes just sits in front of his gate in the mornings and stares. But I don't mind him. He hasn't done anything to anyone." Jazmine added, "Kuya is just estranged from his family."

Fiona gritted her teeth and glanced down at Liam. After a while, she put in, "By the way, I saw Liam's medical booklet in his bag. You're seeing a Dr. Lagon, right?"

"Yes. He's a great pediatrician at the PGH—"

"At the PGH?" Fiona squirmed. "A longtime friend of ours is actually a pedia at the Medical City. Maybe you can take Liam there sometime. I can arrange for the appointment."

Jazmine cringed. "Consultation fees at the MC are usually . . . expensive. Dr. Lagon is a highly recommended specialist. We enlist him for some of our programs at Ganoop."

"Yes, of course. Just that, the PGH is very . . . open to the public . . . But that should do, I suppose." Fiona pursed her lips. "You know, since you're busy catching up with work, like you mentioned last time . . ."

Jazmine watched as Fiona stood up and bounced Liam in her arms.

"You can leave Liam with me during the weekdays. That way you can get as much sleep as you need and focus on work."

Jazmine gaped at her. For what seemed like several minutes.

"J-just an offer." Fiona waved a hand in the air. "'Cause

Sitti looks after him at night . . . You can choose to do it on some weeks. Just whenever you need it."

Jazmine nodded, taking in her words.

Wow, that's a generous offer. Five whole days. Just by myself. I can arrange meetings with more potential sponsors if I don't need to be home on the dot. And that work plan for the medical mission. Is it too much to hope that I can get promoted this year? Jumping to the next pay grade would really help Liam and me.

When Jazmine got lost in her thoughts and stared blankly ahead, Fiona let out a nervous chuckle. "Oh, don't get too stressed about it, Jazmine."

Jazmine shook her head. "Of course, Tita. I'll . . . I'll think about it. Probably not every week. Just once in a while."

"Of course, of course."

Both women kissed each other on the cheeks goodbye.

The next day, after she had fetched Liam and brought him home, Jazmine studied her son as he slept in his crib. His little chest moved with the breaths he took. Once, his hand gave a little quiver as he inhaled deeply. His arms had grown rounder, and the lines on his wrists had become more pronounced.

They're letting him drink more milk than he should.

Jazmine sighed and shook her head at herself.

Be grateful. He's going to shed the extra weight once he starts walking anyway.

The lullaby music played at the right volume, the shine from the night-light did not stray near her baby's face, and the baby monitor faced the crib. And so she stepped out of the room and joined her friends at the dining table.

The other girls were still clad in formal office wear: Anne donned a metallic midi with a black overlay, Zara relaxed in pale pink peg trousers and a grey tunic wrap top, Laine tidied up the table in a champagne floral jacquard dress, while Jazmine treaded around her apartment in a black nursing tank and olive cargo shorts. They had finished dinner, easily polishing off the Bugong roast chicken.

"So how was it at Tita's?" Anne asked and gritted her teeth.

Laine nudged Anne in the ribs before clearing the table.

"I'm asking nicely," Anne retorted.

"He was good. They managed well," Jazmine answered as she sat down on the chair across Anne.

Anne shrugged. "That's good."

"Umm . . . Tita offered to take Liam during the weekdays," Jazmine shared.

Zara's eyes narrowed. "You mean, all of the weekdays?"

Jazmine nodded slowly. The air in the room thickened as Anne and Zara regarded each other, and then Zara quickly looked away. Laine huffed a breath. Jazmine's heartbeat began to race. Her eyes darted to Anne.

Anne clenched her teeth. "This arrangement with her is starting to smell fishy."

"Anne . . . ," Zara warned.

Laine let out a sigh.

Jazmine's mouth dropped open. "I know you're not in favor of my arrangement with her. But what are you talking about?"

Anne declared, "She's trying to take control of Liam."

"She's not trying to take control of anything. She's been helping me a lot. I've been able to function better since Liam was born."

"Jaz, please. You can't let Liam spend more time with her," Anne argued. "Five days . . . that's more days than there are on the weekend."

I didn't share this with them just to argue.

"Why not?" Jazmine retorted. "She's his grandmother."

87

"Tell me. Does she follow everything you tell her to do?" Anne countered. "How much sleep he should get? What toys he should play with?"

Jazmine stuttered, "Sh-she's entitled to make changes, because she's taking care of him for days."

"C'mon, Jaz. We all know how picky you are about things in the house. I almost went crazy the first time you taught me how to wash his bottles."

"She's his grandmother!" Jazmine stood up from her seat. "She's his family."

"Right." Anne glared. "And remind yourself that she isn't yours."

Jazmine gasped.

"Anne, stop," Laine whispered and laid a hand on Anne's shoulders.

Anne scowled at Jazmine. "Remember that you don't owe her anything. He's your child. You're his only parent. Don't sell that away."

Jazmine trembled as Anne's words hit her. She closed her eyes and took a deep breath. "That's easy for you to say." Her eyes flew open. "Because you've never been awake for twenty-four hours, around the clock. I need to breathe too."

"For five days? At what cost? Before you know it, she'll be telling you how to take care of him."

"You don't understand!" Jazmine clenched her fists. "I have to work so that I can provide for my son! Okay?" Jazmine cursed. "Back home, people leave their children with the grandparents, so that they can go to the city and work. That's an acceptable reality for me. It might not be for you, because you can afford help. With your high-paying job—which, by the way, is simply about scoring money for your company and yourself!"

Anne glowered and stood up.

"Anne, sit down!" Zara commanded and pulled her friend back to her seat. "Let's not fight over this. We're all tired. It's been a long week. Let's take a breather."

"Laine?" Jazmine's head snapped toward Laine, and Jazmine raised her eyebrows. "What do you think about this?"

Laine sighed and glanced at Zara for help. Zara simply shook her head and looked away.

"Honestly, Jaz . . . I don't feel good about this. I have relatives who leave their children in the province too . . . but the relationship with their parents . . . isn't that great—"

Jazmine cursed again and turned away.

"Jaz, you can do this. Getting help a couple of days a week is good enough. Ate Helen comes over anyway when Liam is here . . . ," Laine urged. "It's better for Liam to be with you. I can help out more, if you need me."

Jazmine shook her head and glared at Laine. At this, Laine's shoulders slumped.

Jazmine pointed a finger at Anne. "I can't believe you're taking her side on this!"

"I'm not taking her side!" Laine insisted. "This is what I wish for you and Liam."

Jazmine shook her head. "But you know that I'm struggling here."

"The first few years will be tough, but it'll get better."

Jazmine clenched her fists and turned to Zara. "And you?"

"I honestly don't know, Jaz. What . . ." Zara's eyes darted from Laine to Anne. Anne rolled her eyes. "What you're looking for is something practical. And that's completely understandable," Zara put in. "If it were your parents who'd look after Liam, I would say go ahead. But with Braden's parents, I'm not sure . . ."

Jazmine turned around and walked into the kitchen. She grabbed a baby bottle and squirted Joy on it. She dropped the detergent back on the counter as she scrubbed the bottle manically.

"Jazmine!" Anne growled from behind her, but Jazmine did not turn around. "I want to show you something that we came by sometime back—"

"No!" Zara yelled.

But Jazmine did not turn around as her friends wrestled over Zara's phone. Jazmine flung the brush and the teats into the basin.

When the tussle among her friends stopped and silence settled over the room, Jazmine muttered, "Can you gals please leave?"

"Wait, I've got—," Anne tried again, but Zara clamped a hand over Anne's mouth.

"Anne, shut up," Zara ordered. "Let's go."

Zara yanked Anne up from her seat, and the three ladies walked out of the apartment.

The next day:

Anne:	Sorry about last night.
Jazmine:	Did Zara tell you to apologize?
Anne:	Yeah, she did. I did overstep.
Jazmine:	It's my life.
Anne:	I know. And I'm your friend. Don't forget that.
Jazmine:	Yeah well you make it hard for me to forget.
Anne:	Life goal!
Jazmine:	Don't. I'm still mad.
Anne:	I know.

The next week, Jazmine left Liam with Fiona and agreed to

let him stay at the Palmas' until Friday. By Thursday, Jazmine had almost gone to the Palma home to pick Liam up. But when she glimpsed the workshop plan, which was only half done, on her desk that afternoon, she had conceded and stayed at the office late that night.

Patience, patience. Just one more day.

That Friday afternoon, Jazmine left the office with a skip to her step.

She had watched a Korean drama the previous night and had many a laugh before going to bed. A dream of Christine and herself had visited her then. They played *sungka*[20] and giggled at each other's jokes like they used to. That morning, she had changed Liam's beddings and washed them without rushing. When she logged in to her online bank account, she had clapped her hands at the balance and transferred some money to Christine's account. There was no email from her sister, but Jazmine knew Christine had withdrawn the money she sent in the past weeks. Later at the office, when Jazmine submitted the workshop plan, Grace had complimented her and endorsed the proposal.

And now Jazmine was off to fetch her baby.

She stepped out of the *jeepney* and walked down the now-familiar streets to the Palmas' house. She studied the front gardens of the houses that she passed and smiled when one took her fancy. The gumamelas on the woody shrubs bloomed, and the fruity scents coming from the star apple trees did not escape her this time. The neighborhood streets showed little action, as people favored malls, restaurants, and bars this time

---

[20] A traditional Filipino game played with seashells on a wooden boatlike board with two rows of seven circular holes and two large holes at both ends, called "heads"

of the day and week.

Thank God it is Friday.

She rang the buzzer by the gate, but not before she brushed a hand down her peach pleated skirt. The garment was new—she had bought it for a few hundred pesos at a boutique sale near the office. After a while, Sitti came out to greet her.

"Hi, Ms. Jazmine." Sitti laid a hand on the lock.

"Hi," Jazmine greeted back.

Jazmine waited for Sitti to let her enter, but the maid did not move. When Jazmine frowned at her, Sitti merely bit at a finger.

"Can you please let me in?" Jazmine asked. "I'm picking Liam up."

Sitti squirmed. "Uh, Ma'am Fiona is waking him up and getting him dressed."

"Okay." Jazmine peered at the house. "So . . . can I come in while I wait?"

Why is she being weird?

"Uh . . ." Sitti squirmed yet again and glanced back at the house. "Ma'am Fiona said she'll bring Liam outside. Can you just wait a while?"

Before Jazmine could say anything, Sitti rushed back to the house and closed the front door behind her.

What is going on? Did something happen to Liam? If anything happened to him—

Jazmine stared at the house and searched the windows. Nothing of note there. She contemplated ringing the buzzer again.

Nah, Sitti was just being weird. They'll come out in a while.

When ten minutes passed, she leaned against the gate and began to tap her feet on the ground. When another ten minutes elapsed, she could not ignore the ill feeling in her stomach anymore. She pressed the bell a couple of times.

Sitti opened the door once again but this time yelled out, "Liam is coming, Ate. Just a minute."

Jazmine nodded her head, but inside she fumed.

Why aren't they letting me in? Is Tita hiding something?

Suddenly Fiona stepped out with Liam in her arms. "Jazmine, sorry. Sitti didn't tell me you were already here!"

Jazmine glared at Sitti. The maid merely opened the gate and bent her head down as Jazmine entered the front yard.

"Oh, Jazmine, look. He doesn't want to let go of his grandma." Fiona tittered as she cradled Liam. Her usually kempt hair seemed disheveled. She trained widened eyes at Jazmine and appealed, "Won't you let him stay with me another day?"

"Well, I'm already here, and I want him to come home already." Jazmine reached for Liam, but Fiona did not pass him to her. "Did something happen today?"

"No. Why do you ask that?"

Oh, because your maid just made me stand by outside to think horrible things and freak out by myself.

"Because . . . because Sitti just made me wait a while. I was starting to think something had happened to Liam."

Sitti began, "I'm sorry, Ms. Jazmine. I—"

Fiona tsk-tsked at Sitti, then waved a hand dismissively. "Sitti can be a little absentminded sometimes."

Sitti opened her mouth to reply but stopped.

Jazmine frowned and countered, "I don't think it was that—"

"Hush, Jazmine." Fiona let out a chuckle. "Nothing happened. Liam is fine."

Jazmine looked her son over. The length of his hair was the same as when she had left him with Fiona. His arms and torso seemed of the same size and build as far as Jazmine could remember—if not plumper. The orange onesie and matching shorts were filled out as much as expected. Not a scratch nor a mark. Fiona swallowed as she stared down at her grandson.

"Well, you're here now," Fiona relented. "Let me know if he looks for me."

How's he going to tell me?

Fiona hesitated but finally handed Liam over to Jazmine. Jazmine could barely restrain herself from grabbing her son. Once her boy was in her arms, Jazmine kissed him on the head. She inhaled his scent and became awash with emotion.

"Thank you again, Tita." Jazmine grinned as he greeted her with a slobbery smile.

Fiona sighed. "Sure. I'll see you on Monday then?"

Jazmine gazed at Fiona, then at Sitti. "Sure. See you then."

Just get Sitti to let me in next time, and don't make me freak out!

CHAPTER TWELVE

Laine and the Bridge over a Pond

Monday night:

Tony:	What are you doing tomorrow? You going to work?
Laine:	Yes, I've got work. Have a presentation to do that I'm really nervous about.
Tony:	And after work, are you going anywhere?
Laine:	No. Why?
Tony:	Just curious. Are you going out for dinner or something?
Laine:	Depends what time I can get off.
Tony:	And you normally get off when?
Laine:	Around 7, 8 p.m. Why the many questions?
Tony:	But what's the earliest you can get off?
Laine:	6 p.m. Are you trying to find out if I'm going on a date?
Tony:	Damn. Are you?
Laine:	No. But you're asking a lot of questions.
Tony:	Are you dating anyone there? You never mentioned anything.
Laine:	No, I'm not. You just confused me.

Tuesday night:

Tony:	So where are you off to tonight? Are you still at the office?
Laine:	Sadly yes. I'm still in the meeting. But my presentation went well. Yey!

After fifteen minutes . . .

Tony:	Are you hungry? What are you thinking of having tonight?
Laine:	Maybe I'll go for a chicken *inasal*.
Tony:	I heard Bacolod Chicken Inasal is good.
Laine:	Yeah, but I don't have one near my condo.
Laine:	Finally the meeting is over! Freedom! Talk to you later. I'm so hungry, I'm going to rush out.
Tony:	Sure. Enjoy dinner.

Laine stepped out of the lift and cringed when her stomach grumbled. As she turned the corner to pass through the reception lobby, she stopped in her tracks, her jaw dropped, and she drew a sharp breath. Tony leaned on the reception table, looking at her and grinning like a Cheshire cat. A smile broke out on her face. He walked toward her, his grin growing as he saw a blush creep up her face. He dropped a kiss on her forehead.

"I think somebody's really hungry. Shall we go for dinner?" He slipped his hand into hers.

From behind Tony, the two receptionists grinned and waggled their eyebrows at Laine. They looked like they had a thousand questions to ask her, all pertaining to the man in the crisp collared black shirt, slim indigo trousers, and black penny loafers.

Tony rented a car for the evening. They walked to the parking lot and rode it.

"I can't believe you're here. Is Manila now a part of your itinerary? Is your mother here too?" Laine asked him as he pulled out of the parking lot. She was bursting inside with excitement at his surprise visit.

"No, Manila isn't in my itinerary. *You* are. And no, Mom isn't with me." He toyed with the GPS to search for the nearest chicken *inasal* place.

Laine shivered with delight at his answer.

"Can we go to this new restaurant named Mesa instead? They have grilled chicken too. I've been wanting to try it out, but the girls haven't had the time."

"Sure, wherever you want is fine with me."

They were seated outside the restaurant, with a view of a pond and trees adorned with lights. Their table had three candles laid out in the middle. Instrumental music played.

Tony ordered the seafood platter, grilled chicken, and *laing.*[21] They talked about Bohol and what he had been doing there. Laine also talked about her presentation that evening. She chattered for a while about the new program a facilitator was planning and the three big European banks they had approached about it. The presentation earlier was for the corporate social responsibility of Deutsche Bank in the Philippines. When they finished dinner and were enjoying their drinks, he reached out for her hand.

"Do you want to walk around? I haven't been here before, but the place looks great." She nodded right away.

---

[21] A dish from the Bicol province made essentially of taro leaves, coconut milk, and chili

He pulled her out of her chair and held her around the waist as they left the restaurant. Nobody had ever held her this close before. Sure, she had gone on a few dates with Philip and Allan . . . But she never held their hand, never let them hold hers. But Tony . . . even though his forwardness made her nervous, *he* did not. It was probably because she knew him when they were kids.

Laine was relieved that she was wearing one of her best dresses that day. It was a petite nude embellished dress. She had worn it to make a good impression during the meeting. The dress seemed right for their date that night, and she knew it was a date.

They walked along the restaurants that lined the eco-park of Greenbelt.

"So how can you still be single now?" he asked, a smile on his face.

"I've been single since forever." She rolled her eyes.

Oh my God. He'll think I'm a weirdo.

He stopped in his tracks for a while but then recovered. "That's strange for someone . . . as beautiful as you." He brushed her chin with his finger and teased, "Is there something weird or scary about you that I should know?"

"That's so cheeky." She laughed and stared up his eyes. "And must I presume you're dating someone back in the U.S.?"

He laughed. "Only if you think I'm also beautiful."

She dared not answer that question.

"I guess it's because I'm a prude. Nobody's really made me unprudish," she explained and laughed at her words. "I'm very old-fashioned, I guess. Dad heightened my standards all the way to here"—she lifted her hand up high over her head—"when it comes to men."

"What kind of man did he say you should find?"

"Well, he told me all the usual things a father would tell his daughter to look for in a man. But for some, they might not believe that there exists such a man because, well, guys are guys. But because of him, I knew that such a man existed. Does that make sense?"

He nodded at her and held her even closer. His body was warm and firm, and the closeness made heat rush up her back. They walked to a bridge above the pond that led to the other side of the park. He stopped and faced her.

"You don't seem repelled by me . . . ," he mused.

She looked away because she knew she must be turning scarlet. He turned her chin back to him.

"Laine, since you say you're traditional and I've adored you since we were kids—" When her mouth hung open at this, he chuckled. "It's true . . . Could you not tell? I wanted to be around you all the time . . . I'd stare when we'd play at the plaza . . . I-I want to see if we can start . . . something between us. If I seriously weren't holding myself back . . ." His eyes dropped to her lips, and he licked his. "I'd probably be pushing against you . . ." He pushed her body with his to the side of the bridge and held her close. "And kissing you, and trying my darnedest to make you melt in my hands."

She gasped but did not run away. Her heartbeat had accelerated, and she could barely catch her breath. She bit her lips to stop them from quivering. He moved his hands down her back, but they stopped once they reached her waist. His breath hitched. She could only stare at his face with wonder at how this sophisticated guy could possibly be so interested in her.

After a moment, he breathed, "I can't remember what I was saying. Damn."

His eyes dropped to her lips again. He bent down and kissed her.

I'm an adult. I like him. I can do this.

When she pressed her lips harder against his, he slid his tongue over the slit between her lips. He paused for a moment when she stiffened. He teased her lips until she parted them. He slid his tongue in to taunt hers over and over again. He cupped her neck and deepened the kiss until he heard her moan in pleasure.

Suddenly, a group of people approached the bridge. Laine pulled back. Realizing that she was uncomfortable with public displays of affection, he slid his arm around her waist again and tugged her gently to the other side.

"Do you want to maybe check out my hotel room?" He smirked at her.

She froze in her steps and blushed a deep red.

"I . . . I . . ." She blinked several times, trying to get her thoughts in order.

He laughed and kissed her on the forehead. "That was really precious. I never thought I'd make the little mermaid from next door stutter in my lifetime."

She swatted his chest. "We can go to my apartment. I can introduce you to Zara."

Tony and Laine went back to the apartment to find Zara sitting by the dining table and reading from her laptop. Her mouth fell open when she saw Tony's arm around Laine.

"Hi," she greeted and then raised her eyebrows at Laine. Question and mischief danced in her eyes.

"Zara, this is Tony. Tony, Zara," Laine introduced.

"Tony! Your childhood friend from Bohol! You're here?" Her eyes widened, and then she was grinning from ear to ear at the two of them.

Laine threw Zara a warning glance not to give away that they had talked about him, but Zara ignored her.

"Yes, he wanted to see Manila," Laine explained.

"No, not really. I came to see you," he corrected her.

"Guys, I'll take my things to the room so you can talk and stuff." She gathered her belongings and walked to the room before Laine could reply. Then she stopped in her tracks and turned around to them. "Unless you guys want the room?"

"No! Oh my goodness. Go already!" Laine shouted and covered her face with her hands.

"I was just teasing. We don't let guys in the bedroom because we share." Zara giggled. "Tony, you should know that you're the first guy Laine has brought here." She was about to go but then turned to them again. "Not that I'm saying that there's anything wrong with her . . ."

Tony chuckled under his breath, and Laine's eyes grew wider. "Zara . . . ," she warned.

"Laine's the best. The very best." Zara smiled and then finally exited to the bedroom.

"Since you're so adamant about not being in a room alone with me, it makes me feel as if I haven't been kissing you very well." He chuckled, sat on the couch, and pulled her down to sit on his lap.

"You do. I'm just really slow and really awkward."

They stared at each other for a while, each wondering what goodness they could have done to be staring at the other's eyes. Tony thought about the time his mother cried when he told her she did not have to work a single day because her son would provide her with everything she needed. Laine thought about a *dugong*[22] she had helped rescue when it was stranded on shallow waters at a beach in Busuanga.

When she smiled at the thought, he asked her, "What are you thinking about?"

"I'm thinking about a *dugong*," she answered.

He doubled over in laughter. "What the hell are you thinking about a *dugong* for? You're really killing my ego here."

"That's one of the most exciting rescues I've ever taken part in." She hesitated before saying, "Maybe that's a good deed I'm being blessed for now . . ."

He became serious, touched by the thought. Once again, his eyes fell to her lips. Her breathing quickened.

He's going to kiss me again.

He cupped the back of her head with purpose and dived his tongue into her mouth. She gasped for breath as his kiss deepened, almost as if kissing her were his sole purpose in living. She kissed him back but could not match his strength and urgency. She pulled her head up to breathe. Seeming to take that as an invitation, he began laying kisses on her neck and behind her ears.

"Tony . . . you said you want to talk . . . All we're . . . kissing now." She shuddered as a heat that was very strange to her rushed through her body.

He gathered all the self-control he could muster and pulled himself away.

"Laine, I'm sorry, I didn't mean to maul you. Are you okay?"

She nodded meekly but was still trying to catch her breath.

"You're still like the girl I looked to when I was a kid. Your

---

[22] A plant-eating marine mammal

eyes . . . they used to drive me crazy when you would glare at me for another prank I pulled." He chuckled. "Your hair . . ." He tugged gently at her hair and smiled. "But you're all woman now. The things you do for what you care about . . . I admire you even more." He tugged gently at her hair again.

"That's really sweet." She smiled.

Then a question passed through her mind, one that she had been toying with ever since she had returned from Bohol.

"What is it? You look like you're itching for something."

She hesitated. "Tony, how many ladies have you been with?"

He took a deep breath and adjusted her on his lap. "I've had two girlfriends."

"And you've slept with them?"

He nodded uneasily.

"So you've only ever slept with two women?"

He cleared his throat, weighing his words. "There were some other women."

"How many more?"

He cleared his throat again. "Maybe six."

She took a deep breath.

Two plus six equals eight. How could you have been naked in front of eight women? Okay, individually, but still . . . Eight? Has God's Gift ever been with eight women?

She had been expecting this, but it bothered her more after hearing it than she thought it would. Tony cursed in his mind when he saw Laine's expression change. He could not very well explain to her that this was a common number in the United States. That would only offend her. So in his mind he cursed the question and the honesty with which he had to answer it. Then he cursed himself for being caught unawares and not knowing what to do so that she would still be happy

103

with him at this moment.

"Laine, I'd tell you from the very beginning if what this is is casual. But it isn't to me."

She did not really hear him though. She was lost in a barrage of thoughts.

Eight women and I've never been with a man.

She felt sick all of a sudden.

What if I were just another casual affair to him? I'd become just another statistic. Could he be a womanizer, a relentless flirt? Sweet talker, check. Awesome kisser, check. Handsome and sexy, check, double check.

"I've upset you. It has nothing to do with us. That's in the past," he pressed again, pleading in his mind that she start speaking to him again.

"Tony, I don't have a number," she said in a very low tone.

"And that's great. That's really precious."

Because her eyebrows furrowed even further and she was no longer looking at him, he squirmed uncomfortably. He had never been judged for his number before. Among his friends back in Virginia, his number was considered modest enough.

"I should probably go. You're too upset with me now."

He lifted her off his lap and gingerly settled her on the couch. She cupped her chin in her hands, still reeling and not knowing how to react. He paced the small space in front of the couch, with his hands in his pockets, hoping that her expression would change. When she did not speak, he sighed.

"I'm sorry. I-I don't know what to say," she whispered.

"You should go rest. You've got work tomorrow." He gave her a kiss on the forehead and hesitated before leaving. "Have a good night."

CHAPTER THIRTEEN
Jazmine and Braden

Jazmine's mobile beeped. She checked her messages, and a cold gripped her body.

> Braden: Can I see the baby?

Suddenly, she felt like throwing up the insides of her stomach.

Stop it. This isn't about you. This is about Liam.

Despite her ill feelings, she knew what was best for Liam was for his father to take an interest in him and become a regular presence in his life. She was willing to put up with having Braden around if her son were to gain the world by having a father.

> Jazmine: His name is Liam. You didn't visit him at your mother's place?
> Braden: No. I want to see him on my own.
> Jazmine: You can see him this weekend.
>   Apartment, 4 p.m., Saturday.
> Braden: Okay.

That was all. She knew she and Braden were over, that she

could never be with a coward who left her at the time she needed somebody the most. However—and she did not want to confess this to anyone—she hoped they could regain some sort of relationship that would keep him and Liam together.

She picked up the phone on her desk, called Laine, and whispered, "Braden wants to see Liam."

"Don't let him!" she hissed under her breath.

"Liam needs a father. He can't be around just women . . . Who will teach him basketball and boxing?"

"We can learn those things and teach him. On the other hand, Braden might teach Liam about . . . cowardice and irresponsibility," Laine snapped.

"Laine, I hate him, but you know I can't tear them apart. It's wrong, possibly even illegal."

"I told you not to put his name on Liam's birth certificate," Laine grumbled.

"Well, all things considered, he's going to the apartment on Saturday in the afternoon." Jazmine cringed. "Can you please be there with me? Just hide in the room or something."

"You didn't need to ask."

That weekend, Jazmine set up Liam's bouncer on the table in the living room. She had wanted to put on the new zebra onesie that Fiona bought him, but she decided to go with a plain and homey blue shirt and shorts tandem instead.

Laine had already arrived and had set up the baby monitor the other way. The receiver was now by the couch, while the speaker was in the bedroom.

Suddenly, the doorbell rang. Both girls froze and grabbed each other's hand. After a couple of beats, Jazmine moved to open the door. There was Braden, her boyfriend of two years who left her when she became pregnant. He was tall, but today his body was slumped. He was wearing high-cut sneakers, baggy jeans, a DC comic shirt, and a scowl.

"Hi," he muttered.

"Hi."

He peered in from the doorway and saw Liam on the bouncer. Liam was playing with the monkeys that were hanging on top of the bouncer, cooing whenever the monkeys made a jingling sound.

"Is that—," he started, then realized it was a stupid question. His lips were set in a straight line, his eyebrows drawn together.

Jazmine could not understand how they ended up this way. They were in love, in a long-term relationship at one time.

How can he not want the son we made together?

He stepped in and sat on the couch in front of Liam.

Suddenly, somebody banged on the door.

"Is he here?" Anne screamed from outside. "Open up!"

"Shoot," Jazmine said and looked at Laine, her eyes wide.

Laine could only give her a sheepish expression, revealing that she had spilled to Anne. Jazmine avoided exactly this because she knew to expect fireworks when Anne was pissed. She opened the door and let her in.

"Anne, Braden is here to see Liam, okay? Please don't make a scene," Jazmine begged her.

Braden stood up and glared at Anne. When Jazmine and Braden started dating, he was cool with all her girlfriends. However, sometime along the way, Anne started being snarky and almost disgusted with him. Jazmine thought he had just rubbed her the wrong way and let it be. When Braden left Jazmine, Anne actually suggested hiring a hit man to get him.

"Guys, we'll just be inside the room." Laine pulled Anne to the bedroom.

"No, I got things to say—"

Laine covered Anne's mouth before she could continue and dragged her to the bedroom. Jazmine only made out a few words, which seemed to refer to a picture. When the bedroom door closed, Braden sat down again and shook his head, muttering curses.

"Braden, why'd you come?" Jazmine sat down beside him on the couch but kept her distance.

"I just wanted to see him. Gabe . . ." He stopped and shook his head.

"What about Gabe?" she asked, confused.

What did his cousin have to do with this?

He shook his head again and waved his hand to tell her that it was nothing.

"Mom is getting attached to him, and so I wanted to see him," he said.

"You should've come days after he was delivered."

"Nobody told me."

"I sent you a message . . . Or did you change your number?"

He shrugged.

"It takes only nine months for a baby to come out. You should know that."

He shook his head.

"Do you want to see him regularly?" Jazmine's voice quivered as she said this. "It would be good for him to have his father in his life." She had promised herself she would get straight to the point and ask the hard questions right away.

"I don't think I can," he grumbled, still staring at Liam.

"That's all? Do you plan on checking on him from time to time at least?"

"I don't know, Jaz." He shook his head. Suddenly he asked, "Are you sure that he's mine?"

She could barely breathe when she heard it, and a knife pierced her heart. "You know that you're the only one I've ever been with." Her voice trembled.

Suddenly they heard something crash to the floor from Jazmine's bedroom, then a thud on the wall.

"I don't want to be trapped in something that might not be real. And I don't want Mom to get involved if there's a possibility . . . that he isn't," he continued, ignoring the noise.

Her head snapped back to look at him, and her eyes teared up. She could barely take in his words. It seemed like they came from a movie script.

At that moment, the bedroom door burst open, and Anne stormed out, with Laine rushing right behind her.

"You son of a bitch. Of all the ridiculously cowardly things to say. You have the nerve!" Anne screamed at him.

"This is between Jazmine and me," Braden said without looking at her.

"Since you clearly don't want to be around like a man, you better send her and Liam financial support. It takes two pockets to raise a kid, you know," she spat out.

"Not on your side of the town," Braden sneered and mumbled something about Anne still living with her parents.

"Why you—well, it definitely is on *your* side of the town, asshole," she snapped back.

"Anne, it's okay—," Jazmine managed to say before she sobbed.

"You better be careful while you sleep, Braden. Somebody might creep up on you in the middle of the night and chop your dick off," Anne continued her tirade, now raising her finger at him.

He just shook his head as if she were the offensive thing in the room.

"I'll make sure there'll be no other woman who'll let you touch her."

"Pretty words from a pretty mouth," he mocked her.

It was then that Jazmine took a deep breath and slapped him across the cheek. A flinch-worthy smack echoed throughout the apartment. Anne and Laine froze and gaped.

"Enough!" Jazmine screamed in between her sobs. "If all you wanted was to see Liam and you got nothing more to offer him, just go." She swallowed. "These girls have been caring for Liam in your place all this time. Just go."

Braden rubbed the cheek where her hand flew, stood up, took one last look at Liam, and left the apartment.

Jazmine broke down crying, her body shaking. She had never felt so desperate to be strong. Yet failing at it she was.

Tomorrow, I will be a stronger woman tomorrow.

CHAPTER FOURTEEN

Anne and the Skyway Idea

"That was a great presentation, Anne. Spencer talked to me, and it's highly likely that they're going to award the contract to us. I can't wait to break this to Victor," Regina, TNP's general manager, announced to Anne after speaking to the clients in private.

TNP is a European-based software firm that specializes in business enterprise solutions. Anne had just done a presentation to a potential client, which was the top fast-food chain in the Philippines and worth billions. The company wanted to standardize processes across its organization and leverage financial information for executive management's strategies and decision-making.

"He said that?" Anne's heart swelled. She loved her job, and it loved her back. "That's great!"

Her heart was still beating from the adrenaline during the presentation. She had prepared the slides, knowing exactly when to emphasize innovations in their solutions and when to talk gently about the pains the company had been dealing with and which TNP could address.

"Yes, he did. The IT staff seems very sharp though. They have tons of documentation for us to fill out for the bid, to make sure we comply with their internal infrastructure and process standards. Can you be the one to go over those and work them out with the technical consultants? Make sure we do it right."

"Sure, I'll be on top of that." Anne nodded.

The world is my oyster.

When Anne arrived home, a grin was still on her face, a spring was still in her step. She and Regina had gone out for dinner at a Mexican restaurant in Bonifacio Global City to celebrate.

As she passed by the hall on the way to her room, she saw her parents in the living room sitting on the white Victorian sofa. Her father clutched a brown envelope in his hand. Her mother looked at him intently, with her hand clasping his knee.

When Raul saw her, he called out, "Anne, can you come over here for a second? We need to talk to you."

Uh-oh.

A sinking feeling filled her stomach more and more with each step she took toward them. Either something bad had happened or she had done something that her parents were not pleased with.

Could it be the supplementary card they gave me? No, I think I paid that off . . . didn't I? Or could it be that I used up too many capsules from Dad's coffee machine?

"I have some news too. Today—," she tried to change the topic because she wanted only to celebrate her victory that night and nothing else. Nothing negative please.

Priscilla stood up and cut her off. "Anne, your father and I think you shouldn't see Daniel anymore."

"What? Why?" She gawked at them. Of all the things she thought her parents were going to break to her, this was the last thing on her mind.

"There are issues in his family," her mother said. Her father just nodded in agreement.

Anne gasped. "How did you find that out? He just has a strained relationship with his parents, that's all."

"We hired somebody to investigate him," Priscilla confessed.

Anne gasped even louder this time. "What? How could you?" Anger brewed inside her.

"Anne, we're looking out for you. And with what came back to us . . . well, we think you shouldn't see him anymore."

With this, Anne frowned.

"Just because there are problems in his family? I don't think that's reason enough to break up with someone." She jutted out her chin.

"Honey, it's not about that." Raul intervened, standing up as well. He placed his arm around her mother's shoulders.

Trying to defeat me by number?

"Then what is it?" she challenged them.

"We can't really tell," Priscilla muttered, then looked at her husband for support, but Raul just nodded.

What the hell is going on?

"You can't tell me? And you want me to do this . . . just because you commanded me?"

"Yes." Her mother nodded. "Anne, do this for us."

"No. This is not acceptable. You have all the while treated me like a spoiled brat as if I haven't worked for anything in my life. I'm an accomplished woman. I've sealed deals worth millions for my company. Yet with this, you still treat me as if I were a teenager who should just do your bidding."

When they did not refute her right away, she cried. Tears fell from her eyes. All this time, she had been working hard to get her parents' approval, and yet their opinion of her had not budged an inch forward.

She ran from the house before her mother could reach for her. She got into her car and drove away, to where, she did not know. Finally, she changed direction and headed for Daniel's apartment.

I want him. I love him. If they can't accept him, it'll be us against his parents and mine.

After she parked the car outside Daniel's apartment, Anne made up her face first. She remedied the mess—she still looked puffed but a pretty kind of puffed. She got out of the car and walked to the gate outside his apartment complex. A man was just leaving the gate, and she quickly slipped in before it closed shut. She knocked on the door to Daniel's apartment.

"Did you leave—" Daniel gaped at her. His jaw twitched. Then he noticed her tearstained face. "Anne, what are you doing here? Are you okay?"

He checked the outside of the gate, seemed relieved, and turned his attention back to her.

Splaying her hands on his chest, she begged, "Daniel, kiss me."

"Babe, you look like you just cried your eyes out. Tell me what happened."

This was not what she asked for, but she let it be.

"I had a bad spat with Mom and Dad. They're really pissing me off."

She was about to ask him again to kiss her, but he cursed, letting her go and walking back into the apartment. She took in the two-story apartment. The ground floor was packed with a black leather couch, a huge plasma TV with three gaming consoles and a stack of disks below it, a glass dining table, and a kitchen that was hidden by a sliding door. An authentic bachelor's pad.

"This is about me, isn't it? That's why you're here?" he asked.

"I don't want to talk about them. I just want to be here with you."

She went to him and hugged his waist, pressing her whole body against him, seeking his warmth.

"What did they say about me?" He seethed.

"Nothing. My parents won't even tell me! It's just because you have a bad relationship with your parents, they assume you've done something terrible." She rubbed her palms over his chest.

After some moments of silence, he asked, "Do you believe that I'm terrible?"

"I think you're the gentlest person I've ever known. You've treated me like a princess, with a lot of care and respect." She smiled up at him.

He smiled back and tucked the strands of hair that had fallen over her face behind her ears. She took in his smooth, shaven face and his chest clad in a midnight-blue collared shirt. He smelled musky.

"Let's elope. Let's run away and get married," she suddenly whispered.

When she saw the hesitation in his eyes, she began to sob again and buried her face on his chest.

He shushed her. "Don't cry, babe."

"Nobody loves me!" she wailed into his chest.

He shushed her again and pulled her face up. "Don't cry . . . Let's do it."

"Really? You don't think it's a bad idea?" she breathed, expecting him to take it back as soon as she stopped crying.

When he did not, she beamed at him in between sniffles. She wiped her tears away, wanting to relish the moment.

"I think it's a bad idea, but I think it'll be awesome." He smiled at her.

Anne thought she saw passion in his eyes. She screamed in joy and jumped up to wrap her legs around his waist. He grunted at the sudden weight of her on him and laughed, rewarded by the expression on her face.

"Then let's celebrate," she breathed and kissed him on the lips and on the neck.

He grunted even harder.

"Babe, stop. You're very vulnerable right now. Come, let's go out and get some drinks." He smiled at her. "We have an elopement to think about."

Her jaw dropped. At the mention of planning an elopement though, she recovered quickly and stood up on her feet.

"Let's do it in Boracay," she gushed at him, which made him laugh.

He slapped her behind and motioned her to leave the apartment with him.

That evening, she avoided her parents at all costs after slipping into the house. As soon as she was in her bedroom, she called Laine and Zara first, then conferenced Jazmine in.

"Okay, okay. I have a big announcement . . . Daniel and I are eloping in Boracay!"

There was utter silence from Zara and Laine's line. A sharp breath was drawn at Jazmine's end.

"Gals, did you hear me?" Anne giggled.

"Anne, are you sure about this? What happened? You've only been dating this guy for four months, and now you're marrying him?" Zara scolded.

"I know that. He's a great guy. He treats me like a princess," she explained.

"How did this happen?" Zara asked a little haughtily, but Anne always knew how to take it without wincing.

She shared the events of the afternoon, not sparing the details about her parents' invasion of her privacy.

"Are you having a church wedding?" Laine asked in an effort to keep Zara from making another snarky comment. "Can't you at least let your parents know before doing this?"

"No and no. It'll just be a small civil wedding. Just us and maybe a couple of Daniel's friends."

"Anne, marriage is a big thing. If you're doing this to tick off your parents, it's not something you can easily get out of in the future. Annulment takes time, and you can't get a divorce in the Philippines," Zara retorted before Laine could interrupt her.

"Zara, we're sure about this. Daniel and I want to do this. I've never been more in love with anybody." Anne giggled.

Laine put in, "Anne, I know you're a wildcard, and we love you for that, but this, it doesn't seem like you."

"Gals, please. I really need you to be on board this one. I'm a hundred and ten percent sure I want to do this. And I need you gals." Anne bummed, and her voice had lowered. "Jaz?"

"Y-yes . . . of course," Jazmine breathed.

"Anne, we're always here for you. We're just . . . worried that this is all so unprecedented," Laine muttered.

"But you're on board, right? Zara?" Anne asked.

Her girlfriends have never deserted her. Not even when they were hungry, sleepy, or tired had they left her to her woes and rants.

"Of course I'm on board. It's just that if . . . at any point in time, you have even just an inkling of doubt about this or want to back out . . . you just tell us, and we'll fight Daniel off like a bunch of hyenas," Zara proclaimed.

Anne laughed. "Thanks, gals! I want to cry because I'm so

happy."

Zara proposed, "Let's meet up this weekend to plan the details."

"I thought the purpose of an elopement was so that there wouldn't be any need to plan?" Laine teased.

"Yes, but this is Anne's elopement. It has to be done tastefully," Zara countered, plans humming in her head. "Plus we need to get our itineraries in order."

"Booooracay!" Anne screamed loud enough for her girlfriends to pull away from their phones but restrained enough so that her parents would not hear her. She lay down on her bed and kicked her feet up in the air.

CHAPTER FIFTEEN

The Elopement Notebook

Anne arrived at the Bavarian-themed café in Greenbelt. Wooden coffee tables with colorful abstract centerpieces scattered about the café. Framed pictures of its different crepes and desserts hung about the walls. She lifted her nose, pleased with the smell of cinnamon and jam.

Laine saw her first and motioned her to join them at a table by the window.

When Anne sat down, the three other girls grinned at her. They already had their drinks. Zara presented a large white bound book to Anne with a flourish. It had pink glitter embedded on the sides of the cover; a cartoon of a veil was embellished in the center.

"This is our official wedding organizer." She beamed at Anne.

Anne melted and covered her heart with both hands. "You gals . . ."

She was about to take the notebook, but Zara snatched it right back and opened it. She sighed, ran her fingers down the first page, and posed her pen over the paper.

"Okay. Let's start. Anne, which dates are you considering?"

"I think the seventeenth or the twenty-fourth would be good." She looked around the table.

Laine gasped. "That's only a few weeks away."

"Yeah." Zara flicked through her mobile to check the calendar. "Those are both Sundays. Is everybody okay with either dates?"

Jazmine bristled. "I'm free, but . . . I need to bring Liam."

"We'll need to bring Ate Helen as well. Let's schedule the flight around the nap times," Zara said matter-of-factly.

Jazmine mused, "Or maybe I should leave Liam with Fiona on those days."

"No, I want Liam to be there," Anne retorted quickly.

The three girls raised their eyebrows at the bride-to-be.

"What?" Anne asked.

"Laine, you okay with the dates? Okay . . . venue. Anne, where do you want to do this?"

"Easy. By the beach." Anne smirked. "The hotel would have to be the Discovery Palms."

Laine and Jazmine nodded at each other with knowing looks on their faces. Zara jotted down the details on the respective pages. It was decided: Zara will ask Don to let her cover a resort in Boracay that has been asking to be featured in *Biyahe*, while Laine and Jazmine will stay somewhere cheaper but nearby.

"Wedding party?"

"Just us four, Daniel. Liam, and Ate Helen. And Daniel's cousin, Ronnie."

"Photog and video?"

"None. It'll just be us."

"Officiator?"

Zara flipped through the notebook, looking for the relevant pages to scribble in. Anne noticed that she seemed familiar with where to turn. Much too familiar. Zara continued to throw out all possible things to prepare for the wedding, until Anne threw up her hands in surrender and refused to answer any

120

more questions.

"Let's get some crepes please," she begged and looked at Laine and Jazmine for help. "Zara is making me hungry."

Anne called the waiter and ordered a couple of crepes to share. Putting aside the wedding talk first, she then asked the girls how each was. Zara was excited about work. She and Matt had already submitted their final cover feature, which would be in the next magazine edition. Laine moped but denied that it was because Tony no longer kept in touch with her. She shook her head when Zara recounted the night she spent hours lying in front of the television, flipping channels back and forth. Jazmine had already recovered from the disastrous meeting with Braden and now vowed to have a heart of stone toward men. The girls, except Anne, nodded at this conspiratorially, swearing off men now too. Despite the girls urging her to, Jazmine refused to share the incident with Fiona.

After the crepes arrived and Anne had eaten her fill, she piped up, "During the postwedding party, I'd like to do a silly little dance for Daniel."

Laine scratched her head. "What kind of dance and which song?"

"The song is Al Green's 'Let's Stay Together.' You know that?" Anne sang the lyrics, "I'm . . . I'm so in love with you." They all nodded at her. "And then I'll go dance like this."

She stood up in front of their table, not caring about the other people in the café.

"I'm"—she pointed to herself while moving her hips to the beat—"I'm so in love with you." Then she pointed her two hands to her heart and pumped her shoulders up and down to the beat.

The three other girls' eyes widened. The two women at the table next to theirs glanced at Anne and exchanged looks; one

121

actually shifted her chair to watch the rest of the show.

"Whatever you want to do"—she pointed her index fingers at them and poked the air in front of her repeatedly, all the while still swaying sideways—"is all right with me . . ." She waved her upper body to the right and sent winks their way.

Zara snorted and hid her quivering lips behind her hand. Jazmine and Laine still stared ahead, frozen.

"'Cause you . . . make me feel so brand-new . . ." Anne curled her two fingers at them, as if calling to them to join her.

"And I . . . want to spend my life with you . . ." She pointed at them with a flourish, ran a hand through her hair, and shimmied.

At this point, the three other girls broke out in fits of laughter. This did not deter Anne though. She continued singing and dancing, enjoying the moment. When a group of guys from a couple of tables away whistled, Laine stood up and ushered Anne back to the table, but not before she waved at her newfound fans.

When Zara managed to pull herself together, she said, "Okay. Sort all *that* out first." She waved her finger, pointing all over Anne. "Then we can put *that* in the precious notebook."

Jazmine and Laine broke out in fits of laughter again.

Anne pouted but still smiled. "What? It's cute! I want to do it!"

The three girls laughed even harder.

Laine finally managed to say, "Anne, if you do that on your wedding day . . . without so much as blushing red and laughing at yourself . . . I'll definitely bow down to you and praise you for being a great thespian."

Anne accepted the challenge. "Mark my words, you'll do just that on my wedding day."

Jazmine said, "Anne, I really hope this marriage works out.

It's a great deal to get married."

"I hope so too. Daniel is honestly the most awesome man I've ever been with. He's sweet, thoughtful. And," Anne groaned, "he's so hot. Plus, financially stable."

Zara crinkled her nose again. "He sounds just about perfect, Anne."

"He is, right?"

As Anne chattered on about Daniel and his perfectness, Jazmine took a long, deep breath.

Laine turned to her and whispered, "Are you okay?"

"Yeah," Jazmine whispered back. "Just a little tired. Plus this is all a little too fast. I'm a little overwhelmed."

Laine nodded and patted her on the back.

Zara asked, "Do you want to go to the spa a few days before the wedding, like a bridal shower or something?"

"Zara, that's a great idea! Let's please. Let's do it during one of Liam's naps. Somewhere close to Jaz's place."

"Thanks, Anne. It'd be nice not to miss a single thing in this wedding." Jazmine smiled at Anne.

Zara jotted this down in the notebook on the "Bridal Shower" page.

Anne pouted, staring at the notebook with want. "Do I get to keep my wedding organizer?"

Zara quipped, "Only after the wedding. Let me fret over the details. Just . . . if you think I missed something out, let me know right away."

"It looks so pretty." Anne reached out for it, but Zara swatted her hand away.

CHAPTER SIXTEEN

The Wedding Gown

"Zara . . . umm . . . ," Jazmine breathed uneasily over the phone. "I'm not in touch with that officiant anymore."

"Oh, okay. But do you still have his number? Maybe you can text him and just see if he's still available for Anne's wedding?" Zara whispered as she tapped her pen on her desk.

"O-okay. I'll try . . ." Jazmine sighed. "Zara, I'm not so . . . thrilled about the wedding . . ."

"Really? Is it because Daniel has barely hung out with us? We don't know that much about him?"

A long pause. "Yeah, maybe. I guess . . ."

"I think it's all happening very fast. But Anne is so sure about wanting to do this. I don't think any of us can change her mind." Zara chuckled.

A pause yet again. "Okay . . . I'll let you know if the guy texts back."

"Thanks, Jaz!"

Zara put down her pen and grinned at the color-coded schedule she had prepared for Anne's wedding. She ran a hand over it. Pink for Anne's schedule, blue for Daniel's, green for Ronnie's, and purple for the girls.

Now, whom should I call next? Maybe there's something I'm missing . . . What can I take care of now?

Her mobile rang. She glanced at the screen and snatched it

up.

"Hey, Laine! What's up?"

Laine hissed at her in low tones, "How can you ask Jaz to book the officiator?"

"Wha-why?"

"The officiator she knows was supposed to be for her and Braden."

"Oh shit!" Zara hit her table with a fist and cringed when Andrea stood up from her desk and peered at her. She waved her colleague away and grumbled, "I totally forgot! I haven't seen that man in months, and he still gives me problems."

"You better call Jaz. Let her take care of something else . . ." Laine paused and then chuckled. "Like maybe nothing?"

"Okay, okay. Ugh. I wasn't thinking. One of the rooms that Anne wanted was reserved by the resort owner, and I was negotiating with them to give it up for us. Let me call her again and make something up."

She speed-dialed 3.

"Hey, Jaz. I just remembered I know somebody who's a licensed officiator. Let me take care of that, okay?" she fibbed, hoping her voice was cheery enough to convince her.

"Huh? Oh . . . okay . . . Are you sure? I can totally help out with that," Jazmine countered, but her voice broke.

"Yeah, yeah. I just forgot."

A moment of silence. "You never just forget people you know, Zara. Laine talked to you, didn't she?"

Zara sighed. "Yeah, she did. I'm sorry. I was so insensitive."

"It's okay. No, I'm sorry. I should be helping out more." Her voice lifted when she said, "I can go with Laine when she and Anne look for a dress."

"Sure, if you think that'll be fun. They're going

tomorrow . . . I guess I'll catch up with you guys after that then since you're all going."

The bridal shop was small, but its name was big. Brides-to-be who wanted a fashionable gown and could afford it went to Lucy Miller, who won *The Runway Project Philippines* last year. Racks of striking gowns stood by the walls. A white leather couch with a leopard-print throw allowed the brides-to-be's companions, obliged or willing, to rest their feet. Today, there was only one other party looking around the shop aside from them.

Laine looked at the long mermaid wedding gown she had pulled from the racks for a closer look. It had a bateau neckline and paillettes covered with Chantilly lace. She grinned like a little girl, and her thoughts flitted to a time when she marched down the aisle as a flower girl for an aunt. She had a toothy grin on all her pictures at that event. In every wedding she went to then, she would always crane her neck from the front pews to watch the bride march from the church doors, down the aisle, until her father gave her away to the groom. She had loved looking at wedding dress catalogues when her mother was in the dressmaker's shop; she thought the white lace, frills, and lines decorated a woman's body best.

All of a sudden, her thoughts drifted elsewhere: a particular man stood in front of her as she donned a long white wedding gown, her face covered by a tulle veil.

Laine's eyes widened when she recognized his face, and she shook her head.

No, it can't be. He would never . . .

Her hand let go of the dress like it was on fire, and her shoulders slumped.

Zara should've been the one to come.

126

She looked over at Jazmine, who was helping Anne adjust a dress on her body.

She looks like she's in even more pain than I am. This was a horrible, horrible idea.

"What do you girls think?" Anne asked, her smile reaching her ears.

She stared at the full-length mirror in front of her and scrutinized what she saw.

"I still don't get that feeling," she mumbled as she flicked the skirt to the right.

She turned around and watched herself from behind, looked at herself from the side, and then shook her head.

"This isn't it, gals," she grumbled and then headed for the dressing room again.

"God, can she at least shortlist dresses first?" Jazmine complained and slumped on a couch in the shop. She buried her face in her hands.

Laine patted her on the knee. "We still have two more shops to go to."

"It isn't even that. God, this is such hell."

Before Laine could react to that, Anne stepped out and announced, "I'm done here. Can we go to the next shop? It should be just around the corner."

Jazmine stood up and walked over to her. "Anne, I'm sorry. I've got to go home already."

Anne's face fell. "But . . . we still have a few shops to check out."

"Yes, but . . . ," Jazmine started, and her eyes scoured the ceiling. "Anne, I'm sorry. I really can't take any more of this." Her eyes watered, and she turned on her heel and walked out the door.

Anne's mouth hung open. Laine pursed her lips and

watched the shop's door close behind her friend. She slid an arm around Anne and squeezed her shoulders.

"It's the ghost of Braden."

Anne gasped. "And how are we supposed to get rid of him? He will haunt us forever!" She glared at the door, willing Braden to appear so that she could lash him. "She's got to . . . She's got to . . ." She sighed, shook her head, and then clenched her fists in front of her. "I hate that guy!"

Jazmine ran, wanting to get away from all of them.

Where's the main road?

She bumped into somebody when she turned the corner that led to another street.

"Jaz!" Zara exclaimed, grabbing her by the arms. "I didn't see you there."

"Oh, sorry," Jazmine breathed. She glanced at the road ahead. *Jeepneys* drove by.

"Where are you going?"

"I have to go home. Liam." She turned her head and stepped away from Zara's hold.

"Oh, okay . . ." Zara hesitated. "Are they still at the shop?"

"Yes, they're still at Lucy's. I got to go, Zara." She half-ran to the main street. When she saw a *jeepney* with a familiar street on its plaque, she boarded it right away.

Zara could only watch her as she stepped into the vehicle. Something was off.

"So how's the dress shopping?" Zara asked as soon as she found Anne and Laine.

Laine looked up from the couch and grumbled, "Anne doesn't like anything in here. And Jaz walked out."

Zara shook her head and face-palmed herself. "Jaz can't let

this get to her. She'll want to miss the wedding, and she'll regret it if she does. I better go and check on her. Can you look around the shops with Anne?"

When Zara reached Jazmine's apartment, Jazmine begrudgingly let her in. Her eyes were bloodshot, her hair tied up in a disarrayed ponytail. It was still afternoon, but the curtains were drawn. There was something stewing in the kitchen; the smell of pork, chili, and tamarind filled the air.

"Where's Liam?"

"He's sleeping in the room."

"Jaz, why'd you walk away?"

Jazmine dropped her eyes to the pillow in her hands. "I was supposed to be the first to get married among us." She looked up and glared. "Don't judge me."

"I'm not—"

"You gals . . . you weren't there as much for me as you are now for Anne." Jazmine threw the pillow on the couch and began tidying up the living room.

"Jaz, back then . . . it just happened to be on a really bad week." Zara sighed. "Laine was going back home for almost a week. Jake was in town, and we were making up for lost time . . . And Anne . . . She had that anniversary party for her parents." She moved toward Jazmine and laid a hand on her shoulder. Jazmine shrugged it off. "But we did do stuff together the week after, right? Only, Braden kept cancelling on us . . ."

"No, no, no. Even then you were all caught up with your own affairs. You all even looked . . . almost grateful whenever he postponed because then you could go back to your own business." She jutted her chin out at Zara.

Zara opened her mouth, but she had no comeback. Jake had just flown to Manila, and she had tried to spend most of her

129

waking hours with him.

"See, you can't even deny it." Jazmine choked up. "And now . . . I see you running around for Anne like a celebrity was in town . . . ," she growled. "It's so unfair! How can you be so happy for her now but not for me then? Doesn't she have enough grown-up sisters to help her?" She hiccupped. "Do you remember the time when I was searching for a dress in Baclaran? Of all places, Baclaran, God." She laid a palm on her forehead and stared up at the dark ceiling.

"Yes, and I remember I went with you then . . ."

"Yes, but you had to leave halfway through. And I had no idea what to do there by myself. I was so lost. No, I was so stupid, actually thinking we'd get married. He didn't even propose." She shook her head. "We just talked about it, and it seemed like the next best thing. And you gals weren't around . . ."

"We did—"

"And Anne said she would come and pick me up, but she came with that bald guy she was dating. I had to sit in the backseat while they yakked about something that her mom said to her. And they kept making googly eyes at each other," Jazmine vented and rolled her eyes. "When she dropped me off, she gave me business cards she'd picked up, but we never got to those."

"I didn't know you felt this way. I'm sorry . . ." Zara threw her hands in the air, searching her mind, hoping an excuse, a good one, would come, but none did.

"Well, it's too late now." Jazmine hung her head. "I think you better go back to Anne. She needs you more than I do. Just go, Zara." Before Zara could protest, she added, "I don't think I should go to Boracay anymore."

"Jaz, you can't—"

130

"I don't want to talk anymore." She headed for the bedroom, went in, and closed the door behind her.

Zara could hear metal quivering against metal in the kitchen. All that she could smell now was the tamarind, and so she left.

"I . . . I thought of Tony when we were at Lucy's earlier," Laine said to Anne as they walked out of the last shop on their list.

Anne grinned at her like a Cheshire cat and groaned, "Laine, you're so cute! You're in love!"

"Am I? But he doesn't talk to me anymore."

Bells chimed as a woman entered the bridal shop behind them.

"He probably thinks you don't like him because he's slept around." Anne giggled, studying her friend's flushed face.

"I don't like that he's done that, but . . . it doesn't mean . . ." She gasped. "Oh my God. I judged him. He's going to think I'm a religious prude who judges people," she groaned and buried her face in her hands.

"I don't think so. He's probably slamming himself, not you. Why don't you text him?"

"Seriously?" Laine groaned. "Doesn't that make me seem aggressive or . . . desperate?"

"No, just pretend you're a friend who's checking up on him. Like you would if you haven't heard from me for a while."

"Okaaaay . . . I have to think about it." Laine shook her head. "Anne?"

"Yep?" Anne asked, making the word pop in her mouth. She looked up and down the street.

Laine let out a breath. "I really think you should tell your parents about the wedding."

131

"Laine, I don't want to." Anne glared. "They brought this upon themselves. If they can stop treating me like an incompetent, then they can be at my wedding."

"I don't think they see you as that." Laine frowned. "They're just really protective of you."

"They are, because they think I'm incompetent," Anne argued.

"I . . . I don't think—"

"Laine." Anne held up a hand. "I know my parents more than you do. Why do you keep pushing this?"

Because I know for sure that my father won't be in my wedding—if I am ever going to have one, that is—and I wish to God that he could be.

"My parents are not like your parents." Anne huffed out a breath. "They went behind my back . . . It's about time I leave the house."

"Our parents are not the same, but your parents also wish the best—"

"Laine, please!" Anne exclaimed.

Laine took a step back. Anne had never raised her voice at her before.

"I know you're hurting right now with Tony, but can you please just be happy about this?"

"What? This has got nothing to do with Tony." Laine's eyebrows furrowed, and her heart began to pound against her chest. "Every time you push me to do something, I give your advice serious thought. Maybe you can return the favor this time."

Both girls glared at each other for a while.

As Laine's boldness began to dissipate, Anne retorted, "Fine. Just don't expect me to do it."

"F-fine," Laine snapped. "I'm leaving now. I'm going to

take a cab home."

"No objections from me." Anne turned around and stomped toward the parking lot.

CHAPTER SEVENTEEN

Four Years Ago

Zara took an impish look at the freshly baked sugar-glazed doughnut she was cradling at the tip of her fingers. She groaned and laid it back down on the plate. God forbid she would take a bite out of her food before company arrived. She was, after all, here in the doughnut café to meet a potential work colleague.

A social business call—is there such a thing?

She planned on waiting for the media executive wanna-be to arrive before sinking her teeth in the moist cake, but it was taking a lot of effort from her to do so. The girl was late after all. And *she* was the one who wanted to meet at this place of delectable temptations. Zara took a sip from her cup of hot chocolate instead and sighed in satisfaction.

The door to the café opened, and a strong gush of wind filled the room. October made its presence known by the cool breeze and the early sunset. Zara had shivered and pulled at her sweater at the office most of the day because the centralized air-conditioning in the building had not been adjusted to the new season yet.

Which is why this hot cup feels so good in my hands.

When she looked up from her source of delight that evening, she spotted a familiar-looking lady standing by the door, looking around the café with seeking eyes. Her orange

134

balloon skirt and pastel pink frilly top posed a sharp contrast to Zara's black pencil skirt and navy blue Peter Pan–collared blouse. When their eyes met, Zara waved her over.

Anne eyed the half-empty cup on the table and grinned sheepishly, just then realizing that she was a half hour late.

"Zara, right?" Anne asked.

Zara nodded and held out her hand, which Anne shook with gusto.

Strong handshake. Seems promising.

"I'm sorry I'm late. I had some trouble looking for a parking spot."

For thirty minutes?

"That's fine." Zara waved a hand.

Anne opened her mouth as if to elaborate on her excuse but then closed it. She sat down on the empty chair.

"How are you? I haven't seen you in a long time." Zara smiled and crossed her arms on top of the table.

"I'm good . . . Jobless actually." Anne rolled her eyes. "Thanks for replying to my text. Liv gave me your number after she and I talked."

Anne looked at the counter, eyed the doughnuts on display, and grinned.

"Want to get something before we talk?" Zara asked, offering to take her out of her misery.

When Anne returned with her order, Zara started the conversation right away, but not before she finally took the long-awaited bite out of her doughnut. It was getting late, and she wanted to go home to read, before she slept, the travel magazines she bought from a newsstand just outside. One of the magazines featured the Batanes Islands. She liked the way it depicted the islands as an adventure destination with rough terrain and weather–it was a fresh perspective, one that was not commonly used on destinations in a tropical country.

"Liv told me you quit your job a month ago and are interested in media?"

"Yes! It was a lousy job. No challenge at all." Anne waved her hands up and rolled her eyes.

"What were you working on?"

"I was a management trainee at a real estate company."

"Which one?"

Anne told her, and Zara whistled.

"That doesn't seem like a bad place to start."

"Yeah, well, I want something more fast-paced, something more exciting." She flashed her hands in front of her with sass.

Zara bit her lip to keep from smiling. "Well, I'm working at a multimedia company. My department is the one that decides on the TV program lineup, the theme, commercials, et cetera."

"That sounds like fun." Anne beamed.

"You were studying BS . . . ?"

"Management. BS Management." Anne leaned back and tapped a finger on her chin. "I like the idea of working in a media company. I think it'll be an interesting world."

Zara leaned in to study her face as she said, "You'll have to start as a trainee though, if you don't have any prior related experience."

"Maybe . . ." Anne mulled over this for a moment. "I can ask your manager to let me start as an associate. From what I've seen, trainees are given all the boring jobs."

Zara pursed her lips.

Try talking to Vera.

She asked Anne some more questions about her courses in college or what she might have learned at her previous job. Liv and Zara were tight during college, and she did not want to let her down too quickly. Liv had, after all, said that Anne was a family friend. Zara sighed when she eventually found that there was nothing too off about Anne to *not* refer her to her boss.

"It seems our company might be a good next option for you. You can send your CV to my email address, and I'll pass it on to my manager." Zara smiled and leaned back in her seat, ready to call it a night. "It'll be up to her though whether to get you or not."

"Yey!" Anne raised her fists in victory. "This is a good start. I'll send my CV to you tomorrow morning." She leaned in. "Let's celebrate!"

Zara shook her head. "Oh, I plan to go home in a while actually."

"Oh, sure, that's fine. Do you have drinks at home?"

Zara's mouth fell open. "Wha-what? I actually do, but I meant that . . ."

"Perfect! Let's go. Let me grab another box so we have something to munch too."

After Anne stood up cheerily and headed for the counter again, Zara took a deep breath and shook her head. When the two stepped out of the café, Anne had already planned to convoy after Zara's car.

A cold breeze blew through the street just then. Anne squealed in delight and grabbed on to Zara's arm. Her skirt blew halfway up before she giddily grabbed on to its sides to keep from exposing more of herself. Zara froze at the close contact but then forced her body to relax. She smiled hesitantly at Anne as the chummy hugger laughed.

"Where's your car? I'm parked over there." Anne pointed at an old-model Benz parked across the road.

A rich girl. No wonder. God, why did Liv drag me into doing this? If Vera doesn't like her, she'll take it against me.

"I'm parked over there. The red Corolla. Just follow closely

137

behind me."

Zara considered losing her in the traffic. Her brother had taught her how to do that.

Darn it. Liv.

Anne stepped into the condo unit and turned green with envy when she saw the insides. It was clearly a young urbanite's home. The unit was not expansive, but the space was enough for two tenants. Shoeboxes were stacked up high beside a couple of shoe racks by the door. Flyers of food delivery, water refilling stations, and laundry services were pinned to a wallboard above the telephone in the living room. The television was tuned in to a sitcom rerun.

God, when will I dare to leave my parents' home and get my own pad? Ahh . . . but nothing can beat having household help. Not to mention the gourmet meals that Mom is so fond of. And Dad's espresso machine.

Anne pouted at herself.

Two girls sat on the couch, watching the television. The girl with round hazel eyes sat up quickly when Zara closed the door behind her. The girl was in homey shorts and a T-shirt.

Roommate?

The *morena* in a grey pencil skirt and a floral-print chiffon top just smiled at the newcomers. A pitcher of orange juice, along with two glasses, was on the coffee table in the middle of the room.

"Oh, Laine, I didn't realize you were having company tonight," Zara exclaimed.

"Oops! I sent you a text about ten minutes ago." Laine threw her a sheepish look.

"That's fine. I was just surprised. I brought someone as well. Laine, this is Anne. Anne, Laine. Laine is my

138

roommate . . . since a week ago. Anne wants to go into media, so we were just talking about work."

Sleepovers whenever you want, and the television can be as loud as the fun calls for. Maybe we can watch racy movies here.

"This is Jaz from work. She's in clinical research." Laine gestured to the girl beside her, who was taking a sip from a glass.

"Nice to meet you," Anne chirped, sensing a bit of awkwardness in the air, and waved at them.

"Well, we'll just be over there at the dining table." Zara led Anne to the other side of the unit and motioned her to sit down. "Make yourself comfortable. We can pop open a bottle."

Anne beamed and set her box of doughnuts down. "Sounds great!"

After Zara managed to open a bottle of wine and pour them each a glass, she sat down and propped her legs up on another chair. Anne smiled and did the same. She glanced at the two laughing in front of the television.

"Aren't you going to offer them wine as well?" she asked her host.

Zara pursed her lips. "We're not that close yet. I think she doesn't drink alcohol either."

"What?" Anne hissed. "No way. I don't think that I'd get along with her then." She giggled. "Sometimes, I find that alcohol is my only friend."

Zara chuckled. "That's refreshing to hear but a little sad."

Anne shrugged flippantly as if to say, what is *is*.

"Anne, I'm going to be frank with you. You look like you come from a rich family. You can correct me there if I'm wrong. You can quit your job whenever you want . . . Media is a tough place to work in. We work long nights, and people have to argue a lot to get their ideas through. Are you really game for it?"

Anne frowned, looking down at her glass. "I haven't found what I want to do with my life yet. I'm willing to give anything that perks my interest a shot. Although . . ." She paused and studied Zara's face. "Is it really me you're asking? You don't seem very enthusiastic about the job."

Zara blew out a breath. "Well, to be honest, I've been thinking about quitting. I don't get that feeling, that feeling that I'm doing what I really want to do. I want to tell stories and share experiences. I know media does that, but TV . . . TV is just too flashy. We have a face to put on. Everything has to be bright and attractive."

"Ahh . . ." Anne grinned and mulled over this. When Zara raised an eyebrow at her, she said, "Just thinking about what you said."

"Well . . ." Zara raised her wineglass, tipped it toward Anne, and said, "Here's to us finding out what we want to do with our lives."

Anne swirled the wine in her glass and clinked it with Zara's. "Here's to our hazy dreams turning into realities."

Laine looked wistfully at the two girls lounging by the dining table and making wine toasts. She frowned. She had wanted to start a friendship with Zara since she moved in. But with her shyness and old-fashioned ways, she had put her off. When Zara offered her a drink the other night, she refused because she does not drink alcohol. When Zara offered her chips on the weekend, she declined because she does not eat junk food.

Me and my rigidity. When will I ever learn? Maybe I can learn to flip my hair back like a city girl. But what will Tatay[23] *think of me then? He'd probably laugh at his little* probinsiyana[24] *trying to be all grown-up in the metro.*

Zara was always busy with work, usually coming home late and tired. Laine would try to start up a conversation then, but after a quick exchange of small talk, Zara would say that she was hitting the sack and would enter the bedroom.

Laine turned to Jazmine and smiled. Their rapport had been easygoing. When Jazmine went into the Human Resources office earlier that day, wanting to talk about her career plans, it had been effortless for Laine to start up the discussion and ask the right questions. Jazmine even shared her personal and financial goals.

Jazmine talked about starting medical missions within the company, wanting to go to poor communities and distribute medicines to children and elderly people. Unfortunately, the pharmaceutical company they were working in outsourced their charities to nonprofit organizations. Laine resonated with the ideas that Jazmine threw out, which was why she invited her to dinner that evening.

Plus, she likes my favorite sitcom of all time.

"Oh, I like this part! This is so funny." Laine giggled even before the scene played out.

Jazmine laughed at the television screen. It was nice to go out for dinner that night and just relax. Laine was not from Metro Manila but had studied at a university in the city, just like her. They found out that they came from the same alma mater but were a year apart.

---

[23] Father
[24] A woman who grew up in the province; generally used for a woman who grew up outside Metro Manila

If our paths had crossed then, we could have been good friends for a long time already. And she makes delicious fresh orange juice. Who has the time to do that?

She took a sip from her glass leisurely.

Suddenly Laine bounced in her seat and grabbed her own glass. "Let's toast to the start of a new friendship."

"I like that!" Jazmine cheered and clinked her glass with Laine's.

"No, wait, you got to toast for something too."

"Umm . . . can I toast to my sister's first sem at school?" Jazmine chuckled to herself.

When Laine shook her head, Jazmine looked up at the ceiling, willing her mind to come up with something.

No man in my life. Except my good friend Gabe. But then he's just a friend. My job has become depressing to me. What else could there be?

"I really can't think of anything."

"No," Laine groaned. "You're supposed to toast to something for yourself. Like . . . to finding a way to help those in need."

"Okay, that then!" Jazmine cheered.

They clinked their glasses again and grinned at each other.

"Oh, oh, you got to watch this part," Laine quipped, pulling at Jazmine's arm for attention.

When Laine and Jazmine laughed out loud a tenth time since Zara opened the bottle of wine, Anne's curiosity was piqued.

"I wonder which episode they're watching." She grinned.

Zara stood up, walked toward the couch, and took a look at the screen.

"Oh, it's the episode where that . . . that lady there with the dark hair becomes a head chef!" she exclaimed. She waved at Anne to come over and watch. Turning to Laine, she asked, "What's her name again?"

Before Laine could answer, Anne pulled up a chair beside the couch and cheered, "Oh yeah, this is the episode where the men *are going to party*!"

"You gals know this too? I'm just so out of it," Jazmine moaned. "This is the first time I'm watching this series."

"You should watch it from the beginning. It's a great story about friendship," Laine quipped.

"Yeah, it'd be great to have friends like that." Jazmine grinned at Laine.

"Yeah!" Laine cheered.

Anne looked at Zara with wide laughing eyes. Zara just grinned and tried her best not to snicker.

"Care for a doughnut?" Anne asked the giggling pair on the couch.

"Sure!" Laine answered immediately. She had been eyeing the box since they arrived.

"Wine?" Zara invited.

"Can I have a little bit?" Jazmine asked.

"I have some delicacies from my hometown," Laine offered.

A bustle of motion filled the room as the girls grabbed for what they had on hand and rushed back to the couch. Food and drinks were exchanged, as were smiles, nods, and thank-you's. As the hour passed, spurts of laughter filled the room every now and then.

The October night was cold outside, but within the four walls that surrounded them, the four girls, much to their surprise, found that they were merry, that they were snug, and that they were warm.

CHAPTER EIGHTEEN
Hearts Are Tested

After exhausting her body, Laine floated on her back in the swimming pool at the sports complex nearest their condo. The Olympic-size pool had eight lap lanes for paying swimmers, but only two lanes were in use that night.

She stared at the stars on the sky and sighed. If she could count the number of sighs she had heaved that night . . .

This was the first time she had wanted to be away from the girls. She did not even want to go home yet, knowing that if Zara were there, she would ask a hundred questions about Anne. And Laine did not want to talk nor think about Anne. Laine texted Tony after she and Anne fought. Tony had not replied yet, and it had been three hours since.

God, my first time to fall in love and I lose him in a matter of weeks. What's he doing? Thinking? Why doesn't he want to talk to me anymore?

Anne just keeps pushing me. Grr . . . All the time. And I tell her to do one thing . . . One thing. And she barks at me.

Tatay, where are you? Tell me what to do. Might Nanay know? Will you tell me that I don't need him, I deserve better? You know I'd believe you. Only, it hurts . . .

She relaxed her neck, and she sank. She blew air from her mouth, forming bubbles in the water, and closed her eyes.

Perhaps if I calm down, I could hear Tatay's answer . . . Right.

Anne plonked on her bed and scrubbed her face hard with her palms. Laine had not answered any of her calls. Anne kicked her bag off the sheets, let it fall to the floor, and growled.

I am right, right? What does she know about my parents? Just because her father and mother are parenting role models, church role models, socially responsible role models—ugh—doesn't make her an expert on mine.

She heaved a sigh and shook her head.

If I was right though, why do I hate myself right now?

She growled again.

Because I snapped at her. I really shouldn't have. I got to make some grand gesture. She's always putty for that . . . Right? But what? I got nothing . . . I really should pay more attention to details . . .

Her phone buzzed from the floor, and she picked it up.

Zara chirped from the other end of the line, "Don't forget to write your vows tonight."

Anne groaned, "It's already late."

"Our schedule says your vows should've been completed yesterday."

"Noo . . . don't give me that."

"You won't have time to do it this week, remember? You've got that bid at the office, for which you'll be working nights. Remember?" Zara scolded and *tsk-tsked.* "Plus, it's in the schedule. We gotta stick to the schedule."

Anne rolled her eyes. "Fine."

"Less sexual content and . . . more about the future. Classy, okay?"

Anne grumbled, "They're my vows to keep."

Zara scoffed. "I'll edit them before the wedding. Have you

started packing for when you move out of the house?"

Anne sighed. "No. I can't begin to think about that yet. I'll slowly move my stuff to Daniel's."

A long pause occurred.

"Okay," Zara replied. "I'll leave that to you then. I'm just organizing the wedding."

Anne rolled her eyes and grinned. "Fine. Talk to you tomorrow?"

They hung up. Anne's eyes suddenly landed on her bag and its contents sprawled on the rug.

Now what was I thinking about again?

She smacked her face. She lifted her phone and called Zara again.

Jazmine washed the dishes as she left Liam in the *sala* to stare at the crib mobile going round and round. Suddenly she threw the sponge at the sink, and tears fell down her cheeks. Her shoulders slumped forward as she clutched at the edge of the counter.

"Anak,[25] can you come home next weekend and help Christine review for her exams?"

"Ate, I need some money to buy a book. It's for Filipino class. The El Filibusterismo.*"*

"Jaz, I think Liam needs a diaper change . . . and he looks hungry. Oh great, now he's crying. Yep, he's definitely hungry."

I'm so tired . . . Why can't somebody take care of me for a change?

"Jazmine, can you please help me with the presentation? I think you know the client more than I do."

"Jaz, can you train the new girl? She asks too many questions!"

---

[25] Child

Liam cooed from his crib, and Jazmine wiped her tears away and rushed to his side. She smiled when she saw him try to turn to his side, but another tear fell from her eye. She sat down on the floor, hid her face from her son, and silenced her sobs. She rocked her body back and forth.

Anne needs me.
But I need some space.
I've never needed space.
I need some now. I need time. A few weeks . . .
I'll miss Anne's wedding.
She'll forgive me.
She might not . . .
It'll be a test of her friendship toward me.
Now is a test of mine to her.

CHAPTER NINETEEN

Jazmine and the Concrete Barrier

Jazmine went down the *jeepney* and walked toward the San Antonio Village. She rubbed at the back of her neck. It was Friday, but an unease filled her. She walked down the street, with head bent and eyes cast on the pavement.

It's nothing. Just stress from work.

But everything had gone well that day at the office. Jazmine had arranged meetings with a couple of sponsors. She had acquired the approvals to execute the contracts, which were put on hold while she was on maternity leave. Finance had collected the pledged donations. On programs, Rhonda had reported that the Health is Wealth project they held in Zambales on Monday was attended by more families than expected and was well-received.

Is it my quarrel with the girls? But I already told myself to let things die down before doing anything about that.

She looked up just as she realized she was close to her destination. When her eyes landed on the white gate that she saw every Monday and Friday, her insides clenched.

Nothing's wrong. Liam is fine.

Jazmine rang the buzzer twice. Sitti did not answer.

She pressed the button twice again. As the seconds ticked by, blood rushed through her neck, and she cracked it to ease the tension.

Don't make me wait another minute, Sitti!

She pursed her lips and rang the buzzer thrice. Suddenly Sitti opened the door of the house as if she was behind it all this time. Keeping her eyes on the ground, the maid walked toward the gate.

"Hi, Ms. Jazmine," Sitti greeted without glancing up.

Jazmine gritted her teeth. "Hi, Sitti. I'm here to pick Liam up."

"Ms. Jazmine . . ." Sitti took a deep breath but still did not look Jazmine in the face. "Umm . . . he's still sleeping. M-Ma'am Fiona said to tell you to go home. She will bring him to your apartment tomorrow."

"What?" Jazmine croaked. Her heart beat rapidly, and the muscles on her back and neck stiffened. She clenched her fists. "Open the gate right now, Sitti. I'm here to pick up my son."

Sitti looked at her this time, with lips trembling. "Ms. Jazmine, I c-can't. Ma'am Fiona said not to disturb him. Please, Ms. Jazmine," Sitti pleaded. "Just let her bring him to you tomorrow."

"What are you talking about?" Jazmine insisted. "I come here every Friday afternoon to pick him up."

Sitti glanced back at the house and then shook her head at Jazmine.

"What are you worried about?" Jazmine clasped the gate's grills. "D-did something happen to him? Is he okay?"

Sitti nodded. "He is okay."

Jazmine breathed a sigh of relief.

But Sitti continued, "Just . . . just obey Ma'am Fiona please and go home tonight."

"No, I'm taking Liam home tonight." Jazmine reached for the buzzer and began ringing it over and over again. "Let me in, or you're going to be sorry."

Sitti drew a sharp breath but remained in place.

"Get Tita to come out here right now." Jazmine glared at the maid. "I want to talk to her."

They can't be doing this to me! We agreed, every Friday night.

Sitti clasped her hands together and implored, "Ms. Jazmine, please stop. Ms. Fiona might fire me if . . ."

Oh my God. She's not kidding. Tita wants to keep Liam from me tonight.

Jazmine took out her phone and dialed Fiona's number.

What is this woman thinking? I'll give her a piece of my mind! Hiding behind her maid. She said we're family. I trusted her! I left my son with her.

"The number cannot be reached as dialed. Please try again later."

Jazmine's hands shook as she pocketed the device.

She can't be doing this! How can she? I know she loves him, but this—

"No." Jazmine reached through the gate's grating to get a hold of Sitti's shirt, but the young girl moved away.

Sitti gasped when Jazmine continued to thrust her arm out to grab her. "Ms. Jazmine, please. Just go home."

Jazmine glanced at the house. Her eyes scanned the windows frantically.

We were doing okay. How can she ruin things? What am I going to do?

"S-Sitti, if I wait tomorrow," Jazmine admonished, "will you swear on your life that I will get my son back? You ladies won't leave me hanging?"

Sitti's eyes widened. "D-don't ask me this, Ms. Jazmine . . ."

"What? You're telling me—," Jazmine hissed.

Sitti shook her head and took a step back. "I . . . I'm just—"

"She'll continue to keep him from me?" Jazmine demanded.

"I . . . Ms. Jazmine, I just work h-here . . . ," Sitti pleaded her case.

"Why are you helping her?" Jazmine growled.

Does Tita think that just because I'm a provincial lass . . . who earns enough just to make ends meet, I'm going to let her have her way?

With her breaths now hurried, Jazmine inspected the gate. She spied the metal brace that held the grills together in the middle. She lifted a leg and tried to get a good foothold on the rod. She reached for the topmost bar and pulled herself up. But then her foot wobbled, and after several moments of struggling to find balance, she shakily fixed her grip back on the ground. Her heart pounded against her chest, and she broke out in a cold sweat. Her eyes scanned the rest of the gate, but she did not find any other thing to leverage on.

No, no. I have to get in right now. I'll be damned if they keep Liam from me for even one night.

Jazmine heaved out a breath, and her shoulders slumped.

"Sitti, please. Let me get my son." Her eyes watered as her body trembled.

They can't be doing this! This is . . . illegal, right?

When Sitti shook her head, Jazmine pleaded, "Sitti, please, my son." Then she clung to the gate. "Liam! Liam!" she shouted, and the tears fell down her face.

"Ms. Jazmine, please. Just go home now please." Sitti's eyes filled with water too.

Jazmine shook the gate until the grills rattled and the sides squeaked against the cement posts. Sitti could only gasp and, with her mouth wide open, gape at Jazmine.

"Hey!" a male voice bellowed out from the house next to the Palmas'. "What's all the noise there for?"

Jazmine wanted to shout that they were refusing her her baby and that someone should call the police and help her, but she could only sit down on the ground and cry.

"My baby, my baby," she repeated over and over again. "How can you keep my baby?"

Sitti could only take so much, and so she ran back to the house and locked the door behind her.

CHAPTER TWENTY
Rules of Engagement

Jazmine had kept silent since Zara visited her apartment. Laine had stayed away from the girls but could not completely ignore Zara. Laine had evaded questions, avoided eye contact, and, when she had to talk to Zara, answered in a clipped tone. Zara noticed that Laine kept glancing at her mobile even more and that, at one time, she had even thrown it down with a huff.

That Friday evening though, they had plans to meet with Anne, which they had agreed to before the blowup over the previous weekend. When Zara told Laine that they had to leave for dinner already, Laine answered that she still had to use the toilet and Zara should just go ahead. Zara pushed her into the bathroom and, after fifteen minutes, knocked on the door incessantly until Laine came out. Of course, Laine dragged her feet all the way to the car and out of it too.

"C'mon. Quit delaying and come in." Zara reached for Laine's hand so she could pull her into the restaurant.

"Do I have to? Don't you two have everything in control yet? I'm not really in the mood today," Laine grumbled.

"We need to decide what color is best for our dresses."

"I vote for pastel blue. I'll be fine whichever color gets the majority vote."

"We still need to plan the games we'll play during dinner party."

"Truth or Dare. Or Pinoy Henyo."[26]

"Come on!" Zara dragged Laine toward the door, until people began to stare at them; only then did Laine stomp to their table.

When Anne reached them after ordering at the counter, she glanced sideways at Laine before blurting out, "I'm sorry about what happened last time. I shouldn't have—"

"It's fine," Laine interrupted her and continued to stare at the table.

"Okaaay . . ." Anne frowned and turned to Zara.

"I have to go home early tonight. Can we talk about the stuff already?" Laine asked.

After studying Laine for a while, Anne quizzed Zara on the wedding arrangements. Laine merely nodded along as Zara beamed at each piece of news she gave. The officiator has been booked. The resort has decided to give them the two rooms Anne wanted. The restaurant has been reserved—the outdoor area was theirs for dinner. Laine rolled her eyes. The island-hopping tour the newlyweds will take has also been arranged. By the time Zara was finished, Anne was all smiles.

"Sounds great! Wait till I tell Daniel. He'll be so amazed. He told me, 'We won't be able to get this and that at such short notice,'" she mimicked Daniel and rolled her eyes. She giggled and dialed Daniel's number. "Babe, everything's set. Yep . . . Can you believe it? All that's left are my dress and the rings. I think I found the right one, but I have to go back for a fitting tomorrow."

Anne moved to a less crowded part of the restaurant to

---

[26] Literally translated as "Filipino Genius," a word game wherein a piece of paper is stuck to a player's forehead, and the player has to guess what the word or phrase on the paper is. He can ask another player or an audience questions to help him, but the questions can only be answered with a yes, no, or maybe.

continue the conversation.

A waitress came to their table, bringing a glass of fruit shake with a piece of mango garnishing the rim.

"Diet mango fruit shake for the bride-to-be," the server said with a flourish and set the glass down in front of Zara.

Zara's eyes widened, and she shook her head and waved the drink away.

"Oh no, no, no. Not me. That's not for me."

Laine's eyebrow shot up. The waitress looked at Zara, then at Laine. Then she slapped her forehead.

"Oh, right. It's for that lady with the curly hair. Sorry. Where's she sitting?"

"Over here." Zara motioned with her hand on top of the placemat next to hers.

When the waitress left, Laine raised an eyebrow at Zara. "Marriage-phobic much?"

Zara shook her head, pointed to herself, and waved her hands in front of her with a shudder. "I dread the thought."

"But you're enjoying all this," Laine interjected.

"I enjoy the wedding planning, not the idea of marriage itself. It's to be celebrated, as with most things, but will someday end badly."

"C'mon. Your parents are still together, aren't they?"

"Yes, but they're pretty . . . serious. I'm not sure if there's still any chemistry there."

Zara shrugged and took out her mobile. She flicked at the screen for a while and propped it up to show Laine the pictures of dresses she had looked at the other night.

"Which of these do you like?" Zara asked. "Some of these come in different colors. These are all from H&M's premium gown collection, so Daniel can get them at a discounted price."

Laine studied the pictures briefly. "Much too frilly . . ." She frowned. "We'll look like flowers . . ." She cringed. "Nope . . . I don't do backless . . ."

Zara sighed and searched the catalogue for more options.

"You know what, Zara, just pick whichever you want. Then I'll go to a shop and get it in my size."

Zara sighed. "But you don't like most of these. Can we at least pick out three together?"

Laine begrudgingly pointed at three pictures.

Zara smiled and noted her choices down. She clasped her hands together and leaned in toward Laine. "Okay, now can we decide who should give Anne away to Daniel?"

Laine shook her head and looked away. "It should be her father."

Zara put her hand to her temple. "Yeah . . . but he won't be there . . . Are you thinking about your dad—"

"You can give her away. It doesn't matter who of us does it."

When Laine went to the washroom, Anne gritted her teeth. "Zara, I hate to say this . . . but I think we should postpone the wedding."

"What?" Zara gasped. "Why? No." She sighed and frowned.

"I don't want to get married if Jaz isn't going to be there," Anne whispered. "And from the looks of it, she won't be."

"No, she will be." Zara shook her head. "Just give her a bit of time."

"Laine's still pissed. I deserve it. I push her all the time. You think . . ." Anne paused and bit her lower lip. "Maybe I pushed Daniel into getting married too?"

Zara shook her head. "You said, he said yes right away."

Anne nodded, but her lips were still in a frown.

"Anne, you remember, when we first met, how I was toward you?" Zara asked, smiling at the thought.

Anne chuckled and grinned. "Yeah, you were like, 'Don't get too near me. Give me some space, Anne.'"

Zara laughed. "I learned to trust and love you, because you insisted on being my friend. You pushed—no, *barreled*—your way into my life, and now I won't have it any other way." Zara grinned at the bride-to-be.

Anne rolled her eyes, but a smile played at the corners of her lips. "I so did not *barrel* my way in. I-I just . . . I want Jaz to be there. And I want Laine to be happy with me . . . even if my parents won't be there."

"Jaz will be there. And Laine will be fine." Zara pursed her lips. "Let me do the barreling now."

When Laine went back to the table, Anne had already left. Daniel had picked Anne up so they could pick out wedding bands.

"Laine . . . why are you being grumpy and dragging your feet?" Zara asked.

When Laine shook her head and continued to sulk, Zara continued, "Laine . . . this is Anne's wedding . . . We should be there for her no matter what. You should be here a hundred percent for her like she will be for you. And now Jazmine won't even talk to us." She shook her head.

Laine sighed. "Zara, you know that talking to her parents about this is sound advice. I'm not reciting some passage from a rule book."

"I know, Laine. But that is Anne's decision to make. You girls can't let the stress of a wedding break us apart." Zara's voice broke. "You gals are like *my* family, you know. I don't know what I'd do if we fell apart."

"What are you talking about, Zara? You've got family," Laine interjected. "And they live just here in Manila."

"I do have family. But I'm not close with my parents. I don't know where my brother is. I don't know when I'll see him again *or* if I'll see him again." Zara chuckled in between sniffles. "I'm being melodramatic, I know. But it feels like this to me most of the time . . . You girls are my family. You keep me together."

Laine sniffed.

Zara continued with her tirade. "And Anne is frantically preparing for her wedding . . . No, actually, she's not frantic. I am, because she's given most of the tedious work to me. But you never know . . . She might not have time for us after the wedding . . . She'll spend most of her days with Daniel. And when she gets pregnant and they have a kid . . ." She turned her wide eyes to Laine.

"No . . . ," Laine whispered. "That's not true. Anne would never just leave us. She's the life of our parties."

"Yeah, well, she might only want to party with dear hubby from then on!" Zara argued.

"I don't like Daniel anymore. And his collared shirts. That are always too tight." Laine scowled.

"Hey! Jake wore muscle shirts too." Zara pouted, but her eyes danced.

"Yeah . . . Well, I don't like Jake's muscle shirts either. And why are his teeth so white?"

"He gets them bleached." Zara grimaced.

Laine gasped. "Really? Did he make you try?"

"He did once, but my teeth became so sensitive after that, that I never had to do it again."

After a few moments of silence, Zara quipped, "I used to stare at Braden's nose. It looks like he had a nose job."

"He did."

Zara's hands flew to her mouth. "How do you know that?"

"Jaz told me." Laine gave her a sheepish grin.

Zara declared, "Now I think we need to pay Jaz a visit."

The doorbell rang. When she opened the door and found Zara and Laine, Jazmine muttered a hello.

"Hi, Jaz," Laine greeted and hugged her.

Zara frowned as she took in her friend. Jazmine's hair was pulled back in a topsy-turvy ponytail, and her purple gypsy blouse had specks of soil and white paint on it.

"Why aren't you answering my calls?" Zara asked.

Jazmine shrugged and sat on the couch. Her eyes were glassy. "Tired . . ."

Zara frowned.

She hasn't looked this exhausted in the past two months. Maybe Liam gave her a hard time just now? Remember what you came here for.

"I've been meaning to show you something for over a week now . . ." Zara pulled out her mobile and went to Jazmine's side. "I'm not collecting IOUs or anything, but . . . Do you see this?"

Jazmine stared blankly at the screen.

"These are pictures of gowns I thought would be great for you then. Jake and I went to a shop. I was supposed to show them to you as soon as he left Manila. And this . . . I had a draft schedule for the big day. I've shortlisted a few restaurants." Zara looked Jazmine square in the face. "When Braden broke things off a week after, I couldn't show these to you . . . Actually, Anne's wedding organizer . . . I bought that for you . . ."

Jazmine blinked at the pictures.

"Jaz, you know I love you. We love you. Look at this . . . It's that rotation schedule we made to help you out with Liam. We love you just as much as Anne. It just came at such an untimely period."

Jazmine's eyes watered, and Laine squeezed her shoulders.

"I'm s-such a foolish bitch," Jazmine murmured.

"You're not. Things just brought you down memory lane . . ." Zara studied her face. "But you can't let the past get the best of you, and let it ruin your friendship with Anne. You had better go to Boracay, Jaz, or I'll drag your ass down there myself." Zara threw Jazmine a warning look.

This time, Jazmine's lips trembled, and Jazmine buried her face in her hands. Her sobs poured out, and her breaths became difficult to catch. Laine frowned and reached down to hug her. When Jazmine grasped Laine's arm and her nails bit into Laine's skin, Laine shook Jazmine by the shoulders.

"Jaz, are you okay?" Laine asked.

Zara knelt down in front of the couch. "Jaz, I was just being dramatic."

It was only then that Zara looked around the apartment. She drew in a sharp breath when she saw a chair turned over by the dining table and shards of glass on the floor.

Zara reached for Jazmine's face and demanded, "Jaz, what happened here?"

"F-Fiona . . . ," Jazmine cried.

"What about her?"

"Sh-she won't give . . . L-Liam . . . back."

"What?" Zara exclaimed.

"T-to me . . ." Jazmine sucked in a breath.

In between gulps of air, Jazmine shared how Sitti refused to let her through the gate and how Fiona could not be contacted.

Laine exclaimed, "This can't be happening."

160

"Shit!" Zara stood up. "Laine, call Anne. This is . . . Shit!" She glanced at Jazmine, who now shook. "Jaz? Jaz, calm down. We'll fix this. We'll fix this, okay?"

Laine nodded her head as she listened to Anne over the phone. "Oh man." She put a hand to her hip and shook her head. "Oh man."

"What is it?" Zara asked.

"Anne's lawyer said if we plan to bring this to court, Tita might tell the police that Jaz hasn't been taking care of Liam. That she's been helping Jaz out for the past months." Laine swallowed. "Tita might say that Jazmine is financially unstable."

Zara cursed. "But Jaz is Liam's mother. Tita can't keep him from her just because."

"The lawyer said we can file a case against Tita and demand Liam back," Laine relayed and put Anne on speakerphone. Laine turned to look at Jazmine, who whimpered at this.

"I don't want to go to court. I don't have money for that kind of thing," Jazmine refuted. "I-I told Tita stuff about my work—even my salary. She made me talk. I thought we were becoming f-friends. I never considered that she'd fish for info to use it against me. She even asked me"—Jazmine shuddered—"about Kuya Red Eyes. Somehow she remembered him from Braden's stories."

"Ja-az . . . ," Zara groaned.

"How could you fall for her act, Abaya?" Anne cursed. "I want to slap you right now!"

"I want to slap me too," Jazmine murmured. Suddenly she gasped. "I-I can tell Braden that Liam isn't his! He'll tell Tita to give Liam back to me."

"No. Don't. Because that's not true," Laine answered and

took a deep breath. "I think . . . we should break in and get Liam out."

"What?" Zara exclaimed. "Have you gone nuts? Break in?"

Jazmine stiffened on the couch, and her eyes widened. "Laine, that's against the law. I can't ask you guys to do that for me."

"I love it!" Anne cheered from the other end of the line. "I'm in."

"It is against the law . . . I don't know what I'm suggesting really . . ." Laine shook her head. "If there's anything I've learned lately is that I let things slip through my fingers. I'm already twenty-five, and yet I'm still dillydallying. I need to take more control of things . . . in my life. Liam is my godson, and I don't want him to be . . . held captive. He's not where he's supposed to be."

Anne concurred, "I'm totally with Laine on this. We should act fast. We don't know what Tita has planned. For all we know, she might move Liam to another location. Knowing the success rate of the police, we have to take matters into our own hands."

Zara cursed yet again. "What if we get caught?"

"Look. It's likely that they will see us as we try to get Liam. The important thing is that we get in and we get out. If they see us trespassing—and they would want to sue—Jazmine would still have full custody rights of Liam, and he would already be with her. They won't be able to get him back."

"You girls don't need to trespass. I can go in myself," Jazmine retorted. "I don't want to get y-you into trouble."

"Shut up, Abaya. Don't think we'll let you go to battle solo. I'm coming over." A jingle of keys came from Anne's end of the line. "In the meantime, draw the layout of their property. We have to find a way to get in."

CHAPTER TWENTY-ONE

When Girls Go Marching In

"So we're going to the Palma residence today at 2:00 p.m., *siesta*[27] time. The less people in the house, the better. If they're napping, that'd be the best." Anne clapped her hands. "This morning, we need to prepare our bodies. Let's stretch, make sure we can lunge and jump when we need to."

"Sure, sure." Jazmine clapped her hands as she jogged in place.

It was ten o'clock that Saturday morning. The girls met on the long spread of grass in the Ilang-Ilang Garden of the Loyola Park. The sunlight struck the ground from directly above, and so the girls chose a spot under a narra tree.

When Zara saw someone at the other end of the field wave at their direction, she squinted. "Who's that?"

Anne turned around. "That's Zack. He's going to teach us some self-defense, okay?"

"What?" Zara's mouth dropped open. "You've let him in on our plan?"

"No." Anne waved a hand. "He doesn't need to know about that. All he knows is that we're learning self-defense. So don't say a word." She laid a finger on her lips. "We wouldn't want him to be implicated if this turns sour."

---

[27] An afternoon rest or nap

Zara groaned.

"Gals, I'm sorry you've been dragged into my mess." Jazmine looked at each of them. "I really will understand if you back out."

"No, Jaz, I'm all for going this afternoon. But this? Who are we supposed to defend ourselves from?" Zara winced. "Tita?"

"Look. They might have a driver we don't know about. Tito or Braden might be there. Who knows?" Anne argued. "We've got to be mentally prepared for anything."

Laine nodded her head slowly. "Fine. Let's get this over with. I want to get Liam safe and sound. And I'd want us to go home tonight, scot-free."

The girls nodded.

"Our family lawyer will be able to represent us. If anything goes wrong," Anne added. "Don't worry."

Zara gawked at her.

Just then, Zack came up behind Anne. "Hi, girls! Stretched already?"

The girls nodded.

Zack wore a black jersey muscle shirt and a pair of black striped training pants, baring his ripped biceps. When Zack and Anne high-fived as a greeting, Laine, Zara, and Jazmine smirked at one another. At the gym, Zack had a way of dropping clients to attend to Anne.

Zack turned to the group. "So, uh, Anne asked me to teach you guys some street combat self-defense?"

The girls nodded.

"Have you girls gone to a class before?" Zack laid his backpack on the ground.

Except for Anne, the answer was no. Zack nodded and stood in front of the group.

"Street combat is different from martial arts. It's adapted

164

from different forms of martial arts so that if you get into a bad situation on the street, you'd know the right moves, whether you're standing up, brought down to the ground, or choked—enough to get you out."

The girls nodded.

"Since it's your first class, I'll teach you the basics: the palm strike, the chasse kick, and eye pokes," Zack continued, executing the pose for each of the moves.

"What about grappling?" Anne asked and began jogging in place.

"It's too early for you to learn grappling." Zack frowned. "I can teach you the basics this morning. If you want to learn any more, I'm holding a class at the gym on Tuesday evening."

"Uh, no, it's okay." Anne let out a shaky chuckle and began doing lunges. "No need for grappling today then. What about chokeholds?"

Laine cringed and made a face. "Do we really need to learn that?"

"We have to be prepared," Anne hissed.

Zack peered at them. "Uh, prepared for what exactly?"

"You know . . . attacks and stuff." Anne shrugged and began doing jumping jacks.

"We can learn a bit of chokeholds . . ." Zack studied Anne for a while. He crossed his arms in front of his chest. "Anne, you seem hyper."

Anne stopped moving her feet. Her eyes widened. "No, I don't. I mean, I'm not."

Zack frowned and looked her up and down. "Something's up with you."

"No. Nothing. There's nothing up with me." Anne shook her head.

"I don't buy that."

Anne fidgeted and turned to the other girls for help. They merely gave her a look of helplessness, and she groaned and frowned at Zack. "Ugh, why do you have to know me so well?" Her shoulders slumped, and she heaved a sigh. "There's something we need to do. That's why we need you to teach us how to defend ourselves."

"What do you need to do?" Zack looked at the rest of the girls.

Zara stared at the ground. Laine looked away. Jazmine clasped her hands in front of her and begged him with her eyes to take pity on them.

"It's better that you don't know," Anne replied.

"What is it?" Zack pressed. "I can't be teaching you these things if it's for the wrong reasons."

Anne cursed. "We're not doing anything wrong . . . It might be illegal, but it's not wrong."

"Anne, anything illegal is wrong." Zack placed his hands on his hips.

Anne nodded and sighed. "It's something we have to do."

"Then tell me."

"Jazmine's son is being kept from her . . . by the mother of her ex. We're going to break into the grandmother's house and get our baby back."

Zack reddened. "What?"

Anne told him the gist of the story. Zack cursed and looked down at the ground.

"Who knows about this?" Zack asked.

"Just us girls, and now you."

He nodded his head. "Does your boyfriend know about this? Is he going with you?"

Anne's mouth dropped open. "N-no." She shook her head as the thought of Daniel came to her. "Why didn't I think of

166

Daniel? W-we didn't mean to tell you either actually. It was supposed to be just us girls. But we need to learn how to fight if we have to, and you know better than anyone else I know."

This time, the veins on his neck bulged.

"What the hell are you thinking, Anne?" He seethed. "This was your idea, wasn't it?"

Anne gasped and glared at him. "No, it wasn't, although I agreed with it right away. And if it were, why does it sound like you're insulting me?"

Zara pulled Laine and Jazmine back by the shoulders. She whispered to them, "I think we better give them some space."

As Zack and Anne argued, the girls inched backward and sat on the ground. Zara's eyebrows shot up when Zack placed his phone against his ear and gestured for Anne to quiet down.

"Do you think he's calling people?" Jazmine covered her face with her hands and groaned, "I really don't want any more people in on this."

Laine patted Jazmine's hand.

"I should've listened to you gals from the first time Tita called me. If—" Jazmine swallowed as she watched Anne grab for Zack's mobile. "This never would've happened."

"We're getting Liam back," Zara consoled her friend.

Their heads snapped up when they heard Zack swear. He stared at the ground for a while, making the girls squirm and look at each other questioningly.

He cursed yet again and then asked, "What time are you going there?"

Anne's face softened. "At . . . at two."

"I'll go with you," he declared.

Anne launched herself forward and wrapped her arms around him. Zack took a step back as Anne's weight fell on him.

"I'm going in with you." He patted Anne on the back.

"W-what?" Anne croaked.

"No, no. Wait." Jazmine shook her head. "Zack, I don't want to get another person involved in this. Things might not turn out as we planned."

"You girls should worry about yourselves more than about me," Zack insisted.

Anne shook her head. "No, you shouldn't go in with us. Stay in the car. If anything happens, I'll call you."

Zack raised a hand. "This is not up for discussion. It's either I go in with you, or I'm stopping you from going there."

"Don't you dare," Anne called out. "Our plan is solid enough as it is."

Zack looked up at the sky, closed his eyes, and rubbed his face with his hands. "Fine!" he barked. "Make me a backup plan." He stared at Anne for a moment, then mumbled, "I'm just a backup plan."

Zack demonstrated the most common attacks on the street. Then he taught them the simple punches and kicks and made them practice with one another.

After two hours, Zack spoke to the group, "A lot of times, even when people have learned to protect themselves, when they're attacked, they're unable to react. Any idea why?"

"Umm . . . things happen too fast?" Laine offered. "Like how you showed us earlier?"

"That's one thing." Zack nodded. "Also, there's a shock factor. People who've never been hit before get shocked the first time they're hit. Their first instinct is to back down and be afraid. So . . . so that you don't get shocked when somebody attacks you, you have to know how it feels to be hit."

"Okay . . ." Laine frowned.

"Now, I don't want to hit any of you. Anne has sparred several times at the gym and knows how jarring a hit can be . . . So Anne will have to hit you girls. Just on the jaw, okay?"

Laine gasped. "That can't be good."

Anne smirked and cracked her knuckles. "I'd be happy to."

Zara groaned, "Please don't break anything on my face."

"Anne, hit just enough to make an impact," Zack instructed. "Girls, bite down, so that you don't break any teeth."

Anne went to Zara, who was the nearest, and struck a palm to Zara's face. "Stop calling me at twelve midnight just to ask me another thing about the wedding, obsessive freak."

"Whoa!" Zara winced as she stumbled back. "That's dizzying."

Next was Laine.

"Stop being a wuss. Call Tony up already."

"Ouch!" Laine exclaimed.

Then it was Jazmine's turn.

"Trust me more next time, okay? Know-it-all."

Jazmine scowled as she rubbed a palm over her jaw. "What's with the trash talk?"

Zack scratched his head. "Yeah . . . I don't think it was necessary either."

"That was just for fun." Anne grinned at them.

"So who's getting married this time?" Zack asked.

Zack parked the car at one end of the Calamansi Street. Nobody was out and about. Only the birds chirped as they flew their way over the trees.

"It's over there—the one with the white gate." Jazmine pointed at the house.

"Are you girls ready? Like we planned, okay?" Anne queried, studying each of them for a while.

169

They all nodded at her.

"Zack, will you be okay here?" Anne asked.

Zack nodded. He looked at the girls, except at Anne. "You all be careful, okay? Call me if you need me to go in."

"I should've taken a shot of tequila before we came here," Zara muttered.

Zara stepped out of the car and put on a pair of sunglasses. She was dressed in khaki shorts and a cream collared button-up shirt. A messenger bag was slung around her shoulder, while a couple of white C4 envelopes filled with blank sheets of paper jostled inside. An arm cradled a box filled with two wine bottles. She halted when she reached the other end of the road, right in front of the Palma residence.

It's a good thing it's a street-corner property.

She placed the box on the ground and studied the front yard. Nobody was outside. The parking spot was empty. She glanced at the windows and did not find any signs of movement there either. She clicked a button on her phone, speed-dialing Anne.

"Nobody out on the yard. You can get into position," Zara spoke into her earpiece.

Anne, Laine, and Jazmine got out of the car and walked down the adjoining road. They strode down Atis Street to get to the other side of the house's gate.

When they reached the side perimeter, Anne spoke to Zara, "We're in position."

"I can't see if anybody is home. Or how many. Listen in first, okay?"

"Okay."

Zara rang the buzzer. When she saw Sitti step out, she sucked in a breath.

Steady. You can do this. Liam needs you right now.

"H-hi," she greeted the young woman, who was clad in

homely wear.

"Hi," Sitti answered back. "Can I help you?"

"Yeah." Zara huffed out a breath. "I have a letter for a Fiona Palma. Is she here?"

"Yes. But ma'am is napping now. Can I take it for her?" Sitti opened the lock and crossed over the threshold.

"Okay. As long as she lives here. I'd need you to sign." Zara pretended to reach into her messenger bag. "Oh wait, I got this box as well. It's for a Dennis Palma. Does he live here too?"

Sitti nodded. "Sir is out though. He had to go to Pasay."

"Oh, okay." Zara shrugged.

Zara's heart began to race, and her fingers trembled as she reached into her bag. Out of the corner of her eye, she spied Jazmine and Laine boosting Anne over the side gate.

Time to keep this girl's eyes on you.

"Oh shit! My toe!" Anne hissed in between breaths, wincing as she bent down to rub her foot. She had misstepped and hit the end of her toe against a rock by the gated wall.

Jazmine, Anne, and Laine sneaked to the part of the wall farthest from where Zara and Sitti talked. They made their way through the bushes in front of it.

"The curtains are drawn. I can't see," Jazmine grumbled.

"The maid says Tita is sleeping. Mr. Palma is out," Anne reported. "Okay, gals, hoist me."

Anne clutched on to the window ledge, getting ready to lift her body.

When Jazmine threw her a look, Laine said, "I can go last. I can pull myself up."

Jazmine and Laine started pushing Anne up the wall, while keeping their eyes on Zara and Sitti and looking out for any passersby. When Anne got her upper body over the window

171

ledge, she lifted a leg over. Too bad, she lost her balance and crumpled to the floor. Thinking she should have trained more that morning, she clutched her side.

"You can sign for both packages, right?" Zara took out one of the envelopes and a sign sheet. She winced inwardly when she saw Anne on the ground.

"Of course. I have to say, they don't get too many packages. And two in one day, wow." Sitti chuckled and reached for Zara's sign sheet. "You just started today? You got only five other signatures on this."

"Y-yeah. I work the afternoon shift."

Zara watched as Anne peered into the windows of the house. Jazmine climbed over. Laine was next.

"So Pasay? What's in there?" Zara prodded. "Thought that part of town is uneventful."

"Sir is meeting with a friend who lives there."

"Good." Zara glanced at the houses behind her. "Seems like a nice neighborhood here. Do you look after the house by yourself?"

Sitti took the envelope from Zara's hands. Zara looked over the maid's shoulders just as Jazmine turned the knob of the front door.

"I did," Sitti answered. "It wasn't bad. Now though, we have a baby in the house, so ma'am brought in another maid just this morning."

Zara stiffened at this. "Cool. A baby, must be cute. Whose baby?"

"Madam's son's."

Zara nodded. "So the new girl looks after the baby?"

"Yeah, I think they're napping now. So . . . is that sir's box?"

Sitti reached down to get the package from the ground. Zara glanced up and saw that the girls had already gone inside the house and closed the door behind them.

"You know what, this is really heavy. Let me help you bring it inside," Zara offered.

"Zara, don't. We need you outside," Anne whispered over the line. "We've got this."

"Maybe let me bring it to the door for you at least," Zara suggested.

When Sitti let her, Zara sighed in relief and took her time ambling toward the house.

Jazmine looked from one end of the hall to the other. Afternoon sunlight seeped in from the windows. Nobody was in sight. She motioned Laine and Anne to the left, where the bedrooms were. The rubber soles of their shoes matched the silence in the house.

"Jaz, a nanny was brought in today," Anne whispered. "She might be in the room with Liam."

Jazmine tensed.

What now?

She reached the door to Liam's bedroom and turned the knob. The smell of talc reached her nostrils.

Liam, I'm here. I'm not leaving you behind.

"If she resists me, be ready to strike," Jazmine whispered to Anne and Laine. "You can say I did it."

Jazmine peeked inside the room and saw an unfamiliar girl stir on the rocking chair beside the crib.

Maybe she hasn't been filled in on Tita's drama yet?

Jazmine turned around to look at Anne and Laine, then motioned them to conceal themselves by a beam outside Fiona's room. Anne and Laine nodded and hid themselves.

Jazmine stepped into the room just as the girl opened her eyes.

"Hi," Jazmine whispered with a smile on her face. Her heart beat furiously against her chest. "Tita told me you'd be coming in today. To look after Liam?"

The new girl sat up, rubbed her hands over her eyes, and smiled back. "Yes, ma'am."

"I-I'm Tita Fiona's n-niece," Jazmine said.

Could Tita have told her about me?

"Can I look at Liam?" Jazmine asked and moved toward the crib. "I haven't seen him in a while."

"He's sleeping, ma'am. Just be quiet." The girl brought a finger to her lips and grinned.

She's buying it!

Jazmine looked down at her son.

Sleeping so peacefully. He has no idea my world could've just been turned upside down.

"It's a little cold in here. Can you get me a blanket for him?" Jazmine requested.

When the new girl turned around to search in a cabinet, Jazmine lifted Liam from the bed and cradled him.

"Here it is—" The girl held out a folded linen just then, and her mouth formed an O. "Oh no, he might wake up. Ma'am Fiona might get mad at me if he wakes up."

Jazmine walked out the door, not paying any heed to the girl, who scurried after her. Jazmine pressed her lips against Liam's cheek. In that moment when she could smell his skin and rub her cheek against his, her breath lengthened, her heart relaxed, and the muscles in her back loosened.

Then reality set in.

"Ma'am. Ma'am, please," the girl pleaded and ran after Jazmine.

Before Jazmine could say anything, Anne stepped out from

the corner she was in, blocked the girl's way, and raised a fist as if to strike. The girl stumbled back and landed on her bottom. She stifled a cry as she swallowed.

"We're sorry," Laine apologized to the girl on the floor. "But this is her son, okay?"

Anne looked around and warned, "We'd better go."

Just then, Liam began to wake up. Jazmine reached into her blouse to make her breast available to him.

"Zara, we're about to go out," Anne announced over the phone.

Before Zara could make Sitti move away from the door, Jazmine marched out of the house. Liam nursed from her breast, and Laine and Anne ran right behind her. The three ladies strode through the front yard and the gate.

Sitti's mouth dropped open. "Ms. Jazmine?" She gasped. "Ms. Jazmine, wait please. Please wait!"

Zara pulled Sitti back by the wrist before she could run after the mother and son. "Don't! Don't get yourself involved."

Sitti gasped as she eyed Zara from head to toe.

"What your employer did is refusing a mother custody of her child. Don't get yourself mixed up in this," Zara ordered. "Say that you didn't see anything. You were just in your room."

Sitti trembled as Zara's words sank in. When Sitti nodded, Zara grabbed the envelopes and the wine box and hurried after her friends. The four girls ran to the car, and Zack drove away as fast as he could.

CHAPTER TWENTY-TWO

The Manhole

Jazmine's phone rang.

Anne looked up from one end of the couch. She had offered a room in their home to Jazmine and Liam earlier, but Jazmine refused.

"This is Liam's home," Jazmine had said.

So instead Anne had asked her parents to have Ate Helen work full-time with Jazmine for now.

After debating with the girls about staying, Zack had relented and left. He had wanted to stay behind in case anybody from the Palmas charged into Jazmine's apartment.

Jazmine picked up the phone. Her hand trembled. It was the call they knew would come.

"H-hello," she answered.

Woman up, Jazmine. Your son is in the middle of a mess. It's up to you to get him out of it.

"Jazmine, how dare you trespass my house?" Fiona demanded. "You and your friends scared my maids to death."

Wow, she sounds so different now.

"Do *you* know how many laws *you've* broken?" Jazmine argued. "Y-you denied me custody of my son for twenty hours. I c-can file a case of kidnapping against you."

I'm messing up the speech that the girls prepared for me!

"No, you can't." Fiona huffed a breath. "I'll lawyer up."

"I've already lawyered up . . . Fiona," Jazmine spat.

A gasp came from the other end of the line.

Jazmine could not resist. "How could you have done that to me? I trusted you. I thought we'd become friends."

"This has nothing to do with you. This is about Liam and what's best for him," Fiona retorted. "He can't keep staying at your apartment—which is so rustic and potentially unsafe." Fiona scoffed. "Don't you think it's better for him to live in a proper house? With stay-in help? Where he'd have his own room and won't want for anything?"

Jazmine shook as she retaliated, "What's best for him is to be with his mother! Who knew him even when he was yet to be born! Who . . . who . . ." Jazmine continued when Fiona fell silent, "I'm more than prepared to fight this with you. My work brings me in close contact with people from human rights groups. Most of them are children's rights advocates. If you fight me, I'll ask for their help. And some of them will be more than happy for the media to weigh in on this dispute."

Fiona paused and then harrumphed. "Well, don't forget. You're not the only one entitled to custody of Liam. My son is too."

Then Fiona hung up the phone.

Jazmine dropped the phone and covered her mouth with her hands.

"What is it, Jaz?" Laine frowned.

"She's threatening to get Braden involved," Jazmine breathed.

They all stared at one another with wide eyes. Nobody knew what to make of that.

Anne stood behind the door to the apartment. Inside the apartment was dim.

Dim is good.

Zara and Laine were right behind her.

After dinner, the three girls had left Jazmine's apartment. It seemed that the problem with the Palmas was not over yet, and so they had reconvened at Anne's home. After weighing the options they could think of and checking posts on social media, they had changed into black tees and pants and slipped on gloves. Then they left Anne's home and went north.

It was now nine o'clock. They hoped this place would be their last stop for the day.

"Palm strike," Laine chanted behind Anne and executed the movement. "Chasse kick."

Zara squinted in the dark and nodded. "That looks good."

A flash of light came in from the window. Anne brought up her right hand and clenched it into a fist.

This is going to be fun.

Footsteps made it through the cement parking spot. Then the doorknob wiggled.

"Look fierce, ladies," Anne whispered.

"Y-yep," Laine whispered back.

The door opened, and Anne sneered. Braden walked in, and when light from the yard seeped into the living room, he took a step back. Anne stepped forward and kicked the door shut.

"Hi, Braden," Anne snarled. "Remember us?"

"W-what are you doing here?" He looked around the room. "How did you get in?"

"When you need to do something, you find a way to do it."

Anne took a step toward him and raised a fist. He stepped back—his face registering shock. Braden towered over Anne by a few inches, but Anne had a glare that could burn and arms that trained with weights and a punching bag. The ladies hoped their number would intimidate him enough as well.

"So, Braden, guess what? Your mother threatened a friend of ours. She said she'll take a certain baby away from our friend by getting you to fight for custody . . . of Liam." Anne glared at him. "Does the name even sound familiar?"

Braden raised his hands in front of him. "Look. Mom tried to talk me into getting back with Jaz. I told her no. I've burned that bridge." He shrugged. "Now Mom just wants some hold over Liam. She's attached to him."

"Well, tell her to un-attach herself. Because she. Has gone. Nuts!"

"Don't raise your voice at me, Anne, or I'll change my mind just to spite you," he warned.

Anne shook her head. "Who does that—what your mother did?"

"I . . ." Braden bent his head and murmured, "I visited Liam one time . . . Mom made me play with him. He and I . . . Somehow I enjoyed myself."

"What?" Laine gasped and stepped forward, but Anne raised a hand to stop her from going any farther.

Braden scratched his head. "Mom saw it. She must've thought . . . she must've thought I'd want to keep him. That we could somehow have Liam . . ." He cringed. "On our side."

"Are you telling me that you've fallen for the boy?" Anne barked. "Seriously?"

Zara and Laine grabbed for each other's hand.

Braden raised a palm. "It was only that moment." He shook his head. "I . . . I can't allow myself to—I can't have a kid in my life right now. I'm trying to build a business. This just isn't in the cards for me."

Laine let out a sigh, and her shoulders slumped. Zara brought her palms to her temples and muttered a curse under her breath.

Anne scoffed. "You almost had me, Braden."

"Shut up, Anne," he bit back. "We have our own family . . . stuff to deal with." In a rushed voice that was barely audible to the girls, he muttered, "Dad made me move out. Men need to be independent, make a name, and all that. He and Mom didn't see eye to eye about that . . . They haven't been good till Liam came to stay at the house."

Braden sniffed and rubbed the back of his palm at his nose.

"Look. Jazmine shared some things with Mom that upset her. My mother has been friendly to her all this time . . . but she's never really been fond of Jaz."

Anne huffed out a breath. "Whatever. We don't care what she thinks. We know better. Just tell her to back off, okay?"

Braden's head bobbed.

Anne raised a finger and continued, "And I want your guarantee, mama's boy. Or next time I'll go visit her in her home, in her room."

"The name-calling isn't helping your cause." Braden shook his head. "You scared Mom's maids. Did you hit or push one of them? One of them was hysterical all afternoon."

"Nobody pushed anybody," Zara spoke up from the back.

Laine explained, "She just stumbled backward 'cause she was shocked to see us."

Braden glanced at Zara, then at Laine, and nodded.

Laine added, "We'll send her something."

"That'd be good." Braden looked at Laine and shook his head yet again. "I don't want this drama, okay? Liam is Jazmine's. I don't want anything tying me down."

"We'll be working on getting your name off his birth certificate," Zara spoke up, raising an eyebrow at Braden.

Braden threw up his hands and shrugged.

"Make it clear to your mother," Anne rasped. "Plus we want

you to sign papers."

Anne help up a hand, to which Laine passed a set of papers they had acquired from the lawyer. Anne had them drawn up that morning in case they could not retrieve Liam.

"These are legal papers relinquishing all claims or rights you might have to Liam."

Braden glared at them.

Anne sneered, "Don't worry. Signing this isn't an admission that you *are* the biological father of Liam. If you sign these, we'll leave."

Braden leaned against the table and, looking down, nodded his head.

The girls headed for Jazmine's house and told her what happened with Braden. They left out the part about Braden's one-time episode of paternal instincts. Jazmine cried and hugged all three of her friends. Liam was now all hers again. And the door had now closed—firmly, unarguably, and irrevocably—for her and Braden.

CHAPTER TWENTY-THREE

Zara and Matt

Zara pressed her fingers against her temples as she studied the wedding plan on her desk.

This event has to go perfectly. After all that's happened. Everybody's chummy with each other again, but everybody's still so distracted with their own troubles. The beach will help everyone relax, and we can be ourselves again—

Her phone rang. Her eyebrows shot up when she saw who called.

She hunched her shoulders over the desk. "Hi, Daniel," she answered.

"Hey, Zara," Daniel greeted. Then silence ensued. "Anne mentioned what you ladies had to do over the weekend."

She cleared her throat and replied, "Oh, yes. We . . . we had to get Liam back from his grandparents. Is that what you're talking about?"

"Uh . . . Anne mentioned that her gym trainer helped you girls out."

"Oh, yes . . . yes, h-her trainer did."

"Zara . . ." He hesitated. "Can you tell me what their relationship is really like?"

He paused. Zara took a deep breath but remained silent.

He continued, "I was just confused as to why she didn't call me instead."

I can't say that part was clear to me either.

"Well, they're just very close," Zara started. "Like, uh, brother and sister."

"Okay . . ."

"If you're worried about Anne's feelings for him . . ." Zara huffed out a breath. "All these years, she's never looked at Zack in a romantic light."

I can't say the other way around isn't true though.

"Zack, yeah, Zack. Of course, of course." Another pause. "Well, uh, I suppose I shouldn't be bothering you with nonsensical questions." He let out a nervous chuckle. "Thanks, Zara."

"Of course, Daniel. Anytime."

She hung up and plopped the mobile on her desk. She clasped her hands together, resting her chin there, and leaned against the table.

"Hey, do you want to go get coffee?"

Zara looked up and saw Matt peering at her over her cubicle.

Sensing her hesitation, he said, "It's just coffee," and grinned

"Sure." She grabbed her wallet and stood up to join him. "Starbucks downstairs?"

"The one over at Salcedo Street. That okay with you?"

She chuckled and nodded.

He added, "Since it seems to bother you, being seen with me."

"Not with you specifically. I just don't want to be talked about that way in the office." She grinned sheepishly at him.

"Why so? You're good at what you do and seem to get along well with everybody else."

"I want to be spic-and-span professional." She paused and heard herself. "My friends do tell me I take work too

183

seriously."

When they reached the café and ordered their drinks, Matt offered to pay.

"No, that's fine. I can pay for it. I really was planning to get a cup of coffee."

"No, I invited you. Let me take it." He held her hand and stopped it from pulling out a bill from her wallet.

"Hmm . . . ," she mused and let him do as he said.

"What's with the hmm?" He smiled, looking at her.

"You're treating me differently now. You used to argue with everything our team contributed or pitched, but last week you agreed to most of what was in the article I submitted. Even Don looked surprised when you just nodded your head." She furrowed her eyebrows at him.

"C'mon, I don't argue just for the sake of it. I liked the final product even though you left out a few things I suggested. Plus, I like your work better than Gaea's."

She grinned from ear to ear. After getting their drinks, they sat at a table in the middle of the café.

"I'm just cautious about what I do and the people I deal with at work," Zara explained.

"I don't hold that against you. I've had my share of people throwing me under the bus. So . . . are you just as cautious with your personal life too?" he asked, avoiding her eyes.

"Hmm . . . I try to be, but that's more difficult to control. I guess that generally I am." She smiled. "Except with my brother . . . and my girlfriends. I'd do anything for them."

She shook her head at that last thought and smiled, relieved that the trouble with Fiona Palma had receded.

Suddenly Zara's phone buzzed. A message arrived from Anne. From the preview, Zara could make out the text, "Daniel might call you to ask . . ."

Zara frowned, and her eyebrows furrowed together.

Matt raised an eyebrow and asked, "Anything wrong?"

Zara shook her head, but her eyes remained on the screen. "It's okay. Just a text."

Matt cleared his throat. "So . . . no boyfriend to be spontaneous with?"

Her head snapped up. "Not at the moment." She looked down at her macchiato.

Sensing the shift in her mood, he changed the subject. "You up for a little game of twenty-one questions?" He grinned at her.

Zara's mouth dropped open. She shrugged, a smile tugging at her lips.

"Funniest fieldwork incident?" Matt asked, a challenge in his eyes.

Her eyes lit up, and her grin grew. "That should be easy . . . Hold on. Uh . . ." She snapped her fingers a couple of times. "That time when we were at the crocodile farm in Puerto Princesa." She laughed. "Gaea flirted with this handsome tourist while we were in the breeding station. When she was about to answer the guy's question, she took a deep breath . . ."

Matt nodded, prodding her on, his eyes gleaming. He glanced down at his cup briefly before gazing at her again.

She continued, shaking her head, "And sucked in a fly. She choked and tried to spit it out."

He laughed, slapping his hand on his thigh.

"We were all laughing and horrified for her at the same time. I gave her a bottle of water to stop the choking, but then she realized she must've swallowed in the fly from drinking and started gagging."

"Wish I'd been there for that."

She blushed a light pink and gazed at the heart-shaped chocolate powder topping on her coffee.

She added with a smile before taking a sip from her drink, "The guy was so nice to try to help her, but then his tour group had to move along."

Zara studied his face as he thought up another question to throw at her. How she went from tense to laughing puzzled her.

Did I judge him wrongly all this time just because Gaea has always been competitive with him and hated his guts?

That afternoon, Zara picked up her mobile, grunted, and then dialed the number.

"Hi, Anne. Are you free to talk?" Zara greeted. "Daniel called me . . . Yeah, he was worried about Zack. You should take this more seriously. You *are* marrying this man, you know." She sighed. "Yes, it's adorable and chivalrous that he's acting jealous, but your relationship with Zack might be intimidating Daniel . . ."

"It really shouldn't. Which is what I told him. He just kept asking me over and over again if I absolutely wanted to get married." Anne huffed out a breath. "You know there's nothing going on between Zack and me. He's my trainer, for crying out loud."

"I know there's nothing going on between both of you. But now that you're marrying Daniel, he has to be number one when it comes to everything—like running to him first when you need some extra muscle." Zara frowned. "That's how it is with marriage. From what my dad used to tell me anyway."

"That's really chauvinistic and impractical, Zara," Anne groaned.

"Which is why I don't engross myself in thoughts of marriage," Zara countered. "But you are getting married, Anne.

I have a question for you—have you even started to pack your things?"

"Zara, of course I haven't," Anne retorted. "Not with my work schedule and all the things that happened recently."

"Fine. Fine. Have you prepared for the first week that you're moving in with Daniel, at the least?" Zara challenged.

"No. But I've prepared my stuff for the wedding," Anne bit back. "Don't worry about this."

Zara rolled her eyes. "Anne, Daniel is expecting you to move in with him."

After Anne made a few more arguments, they said goodbye. Zara shook her head.

I should stop worrying about every single thing if she doesn't pay attention to what I say anyway.

She tapped her pen on her pad and then stared at the screen of her laptop.

What in the world am I looking at here?

She crossed her legs and tapped her foot at the cubicle's partition.

Gaea will look at me if I make too much noise.

She made a show of extending her arms over her head, then stood up to stretch her whole body. Matt was not anywhere to be found. Looking around at the other desks, she checked that nobody was looking her way. Then she leaned on her desk and hoisted her body to peek over at Matt's desk. His laptop was on standby mode.

Suddenly, a movement to her far right caught her eye, and her head snapped to that side. Matt sat at one of the meeting rooms by its glass door. He had his pen positioned over his notebook as if to write something, but he stared at her with an amused grin on his lips. Zara sat down with a plonk. Heat flared all over her body. She cursed in her head and flinched.

Matt was in a meeting with Don and another man, who was

in a business suit. When the meeting ended, Matt dropped his notebook on his desk and walked over to Zara's desk. She kept her head bent over her laptop, feigning utter engrossment with an online article.

Why are you seeking him out anyway? Prize catch . . . Women must go after him all the time. He probably doesn't stick to one for long. Ugh, stop overanalyzing.

Matt leaned back on the end of her desk and cleared his throat. She turned to meet his eyes. He smiled at her boyishly, not in a smug way, which she was thankful for. Her eyes fell to the dark blue mandarin collar button shirt that showed off his lean body. Before she knew it, her eyes travelled to the stubble on his chin and that well-pronounced Adam's apple.

"Yes?" she asked as innocently as she could and turned back to her laptop before she melted from embarrassment.

"Seems like you'll be covering the resort in Boracay soon," he declared.

She turned toward him. "Really? Was that what your meeting was about?"

"Yes, but Don said it'll only be a half page with a photo in it. Wait for him to talk to you about it."

"That's great! I asked him about it the other day. The girls and I are supposed to go there in a couple of weeks."

"What do you and your friends do in Boracay?"

"Just the usual, swim and drink fruit shakes by the beach. Sometimes we go to a videoke as well."

"Yeah, I've noticed you like to sing." He smirked.

"What? I've never sung around you before."

"Actually, sometimes when you're working overtime and you belt out a song, you think you're alone, but in fact . . . you're not."

He watched with pleasure as realization dawned on her, and she gasped in mortification. She covered her face with her hands and cursed.

"I'm so embarrassed! I'm so sorry you had to hear any of my singing," she groaned. "Was there anybody else who heard me?"

"No, it was only me then. With your passion . . . I think I can try and get you a spot in our band." His grin dared her on.

"You're in a band?" she squeaked.

"Yes, I'm the lead vocals."

When she groaned again, he laughed out loud.

"Want to . . . want to go for a break?" he asked.

"Let me get over my embarrassment first please." She sniffed and nodded. "Wait, wait, I got to jot down a few things."

She pulled out her notebook, a monthly calendar, and her personal calendar book. In the notebook, she wrote the stuff she would have to do for the Boracay resort feature. In the monthly calendar, she jotted down a note on the date of Anne's wedding—the same thing. In her personal calendar, she marked the weekend as well.

Matt chuckled as he watched her. "Your OCD is really . . . endearing?" he ended on a questioning note.

Zara laughed at herself and then stood up to arrange the stuff on her desk. Realizing she had dropped her bag into the bottom drawer of her desk, she bent down from her waist to get it.

"Now that . . . that's really endearing." Matt dragged his words with a drawl, smirking at her.

She had forgotten that she was wearing her pencil skirt that day, and she had just jutted out her behind right in front of him. She quickly snapped her body back up and glared at him.

"Shut up or you'll have to pay for your own coffee," she grumbled.

CHAPTER TWENTY-FOUR

The Videoke Madness

For Anne's bridal shower, the four girls decided to go to a videoke bar instead of a spa. The videoke bar was tucked away at a corner of Esperanza Street. It was the first time they had all been here, but due to Andrea's high commendation of the place, Zara convinced them to give it a try. Black and red colors splashed across its walls, lending a modern and sassy vibe. Indeed, the rooms were spacious, hosting leather couches that could seat a party; the televisions were recent flatscreen models, and the videoke menu had a modern look and feel. Zara checked that the songbook had the latest popular songs. Even the restrooms had a boutique look to them, decorated with red and black tiles and brown vessel sinks.

Anne was in a dreamlike state, with wedding images filling her mind at every moment. Zara talked and smiled more than ever since her breakup with Jake. The girls did not think much about it, since Zara was always the most eager to go to videoke bars even though she sang the worst among them—they thought it was just her adrenaline pumping in for the songfest.

Jazmine yawned every ten minutes or so, and her eyes drooped all the time. She had to drag her body out of the apartment just to be there that night, but she did. She owed her friends so much more. Since Anne, Zara, and Laine visited Braden at his apartment, Fiona had not contacted Jazmine. It had been arranged that Helen would work during the day at Jazmine's house on weekdays and Saturdays. Helen was on strict instructions not to open the door to anyone while Jazmine was not around.

It was Laine though who was in the worst mood among them.

They ordered finger food and drinks before encoding the songs they wanted on the videoke machine. Laine snapped at the waiter when he repeated the order to them and got her drink wrong. Two eyebrows raised, one jaw dropped, and a smirk happened all at the same time.

"PMS?" Anne asked Laine when the waiter left.

Laine sighed. "No . . ."

"Her Mr. Fuente hasn't been in touch with her since he left Manila," Zara put in.

"It's not that," Laine interjected, then sighed again, and fidgeted with the hem of her skirt. "Yes, it is that."

"Guys suck. Why don't we just swear off guys?" Jazmine glared.

Anne and Zara smiled at each other. Their usually demure friends were lashing out at men tonight. Usually it was just Zara, sometimes Anne.

"Tonight let's forget about the guys who suck and just have our girls' fun," Anne announced as she picked up the songbook and searched for her favorites.

"Okay. I know some people are snarky tonight, but I wanted to share something with you gals." Zara reached for her bag and took out a magazine. She presented it to them with a big grin on her face. "Tonight, I'm celebrating my career."

It was the latest publication of *Biyahe*. The front cover was a picture of the Black Island in Pangasinan.

Anne gasped and raised her hands above her head. "You did

it! Your boss put it in!"

Zara nodded. "Yes. Gaea is back, but I think Don is now finally fine with me doing a few of the covers or at least some of the main features."

She then turned to the page of the feature cover, which showed a landscape photo of the Hundred Islands and the beginning of an article. At the bottom of the photo were the words "Written by Zara Castillo."

Laine reached for her bag and took out a magazine as well, smiling at Zara. It was another copy of the same *Biyahe* magazine edition. Zara gasped, and her hand flew to her chest.

"Jaz and I saw it this morning at a newsstand outside the office and bought it."

"I'm going to get myself a copy too." Anne beamed. "Or should I subscribe already since you'll be doing the main features from now on?"

Zara laughed. "There's no need. There will always be a couple of copies at the condo."

When their food and drinks arrived, Anne held up her glass of whisky in front of her. Zara raised her bottle of Vodka Cruiser, Laine her glass of virgin margarita, and Jazmine her glass of mineral water.

"To us, to friendship, to careers, and to weddings," Anne announced.

"To loyalty, to success," Zara added.

"To faith, to love . . . and hope," Laine added.

"To my son, to a good future." Jazmine sniffed.

After clinking their glasses and bottle, they each took a sip and smiled at each other. It was a ritual they loved to do on special occasions. One just had to start it, and the rest would follow suit.

"Now, can I please do the first song?" Zara beamed. They

all groaned and said no.

"No, I already entered my number," Anne interjected.

Anne's first song was the Spice Girls' "2 Become 1," which made the rest laugh because it was obviously about her and Daniel. Zara's song was Beyonce's "Single Ladies," which earned some snorts because she missed some notes as it was a fast one. Jazmine sang Adele's "Rolling in the Deep." The girls clapped for her when she reached all the notes smoothly.

Jazmine was a good singer, but Laine was the best among them. She sang with the church choir while she was still living in Bohol, then sang with the university choir in Manila.

"When I was a young boy, my father took me into the city . . . ," Laine sang.

Suddenly Zara's mobile beeped. Zara opened the message; it was from Daniel.

Daniel:	Is Anne with you already?
Zara:	Yes, she is.
Daniel:	I offered to drive her, but she insisted it was girls' night.
Zara:	Don't worry about it, Daniel. She's a big girl.
Daniel:	It is only-girls night, right?
Zara:	Yes, it is! No strippers.
Daniel:	It's not strippers I'm really asking about.
Zara:	Totally no men, Daniel.
Daniel:	Okay. I have to meet someone tonight anyway. Have a good night.
Zara:	Thanks!

Anne raised her eyebrows, just recognizing Laine's song. "I didn't know she likes My Chemical Romance," she whispered to Zara.

193

It was a song darker than Laine's usual repertoire. As she sang, emotions played through her face at peaks of the song, and her voice rose and broke at the right moments.

Zara shrugged, bothered more by Daniel's messages than by Laine's song choice.

When they had finished the food and had a few more drinks, Zara stood up.

"Before we all get even crazier with the song choices, I'd like to toast to our bride-to-be, Anne. You are unpredictable, a wild child. But you are more than that. You're a loyal friend. You'd fight for any of us. You always move me with your passion. I love you." Zara raised her bottle and took a sip. "May this wedding bring you happiness with Daniel." Before she could stop herself, she added, "And your marriage, the days after, shouldn't be forgotten . . ."

Anne raised her eyebrows at Zara. Zara grunted and then took out a box from the paper bag she brought and handed it to Anne, whose expression quickly changed. Anne clapped her hands and stomped her feet excitedly.

"Open our gifts together," Jazmine requested and stood up, looking warily at the celebrant. "Anne, I'm sorry I ran away while we were gown shopping . . . I'm such a bitch sometimes. It was difficult for me—" Anne stood up and squeezed her shoulders. Jazmine started again, "I'm sorry," but her eyes watered, and her lips trembled. This time, Anne hugged her tightly, told her that it was fine, and the girls chuckled. "I have to say this! Okay . . ." Jazmine took a deep breath. "I'm okay, I'm okay. Anne, I want to say . . . you continue to surprise me even now." She swallowed and looked her friend in the eyes. "You are strong and bold on the outside, but I know that inside you're softhearted. I see it every time you hold Liam. Know that even when you head dauntlessly into a new kind of life, we are here to protect your heart always."

Anne's lips quivered at this. "Thanks, Jaz," she murmured, choked up with emotion, as Jazmine handed her a sealed paper bag.

"Okay, my turn. Anne, the first time I met you, I was scared of you." Anne giggled at this in between sniffles, but Laine continued. "You're confrontational and liberated, everything I'm not. Yet here we are today. I love you like a sister. I still think you should tell your parents that you're getting married." She made a face at Anne. "But maybe . . . sometimes we decide what's best for a certain point in our lives. And we deal with the aftermath later . . ." She cleared her throat. "Maybe you don't know it, but you've made me live out my dreams. When I wanted to learn how to dive, you pushed me, egged me, even taunted me until I did. When I wanted to move from HR to working at the foundation, you were the one who told me to flip off the consequences." She chuckled and raised her glass. "May this marriage bless you and shower you with love as you have us."

At this, Anne bawled. Laine handed her a box and held her by the shoulders. The three other girls laughed, though they also sniffed and blinked back tears.

"Thanks, you gals! You make me such a softie!" Anne wailed in between sobs.

"Open your gifts," Jazmine prodded at her.

When Anne saw the black lacy lingerie that Zara gave her, the bride-to-be cheered.

"I'm so glad you're looking after me in this department." She giggled.

Jazmine gave her silver bedsheets with couple pillowcases. The pillowcases had a cartoon print of a man and a woman in an airplane, dressed in wedding garb, and a "Just Married" banner floating behind the plane. Laine gave her an English-style salad bowl made of china and an inspirational book on marriage. Anne gave them all a big hug.

Then Laine played the next song. "Now this song is for all of us."

Bon Jovi's "It's My Life" began to play. As Laine neared the chorus, Anne stepped up on the couch and began to jump up and down, pumping her fist in the air. The rest of the girls laughed and joined her on the couch, jumping up and down and turning around.

"It's my life. It's now or never. I ain't gonna live forever. I just wanna live while I'm alive!"

CHAPTER TWENTY-FIVE

Last Chance

That Saturday evening, Anne sighed as she settled down in the tub. It had been an eventful week.

She and Daniel had their first misunderstanding. Why he had been so rattled by Zack puzzled her. After his talk with Zara, however, Daniel had sworn to Anne that he will not be a jealous boyfriend and had even offered to drive her to the gym a few times that week. When he picked her up after each visit, he asked her how the workout was. A couple of times, he had inquired about Zack. On all occasions, she had responded nonchalantly.

Anne lifted her hands from the bath and massaged her neck. The bubbles were thick, the water warm, and the scents of the jasmine wax candles filled the air. She lifted a waxed leg up and grinned, running a palm over it. She reached for her mobile and turned on the music.

Zara had booked the perfect room at the resort, with a big bed, where Anne would make all of Daniel's dreams seem like mere pickings. She picked up a book from the stool beside the tub. *The Kamasutra.*

Let me see if I can learn anything more that needs to be mastered. My husband must be and will be pleased. I will be the insatiable wife in bed, the mistress he's never had. What does it matter if I don't know how to cook, sew, or clean the house? I can hire someone to do all those for us. I'll be the sunshine in his life, the one who makes him smile first thing in the morning and last at night. I'll make him want me, obsess about me. Oh yes, he'll never look at another woman again.

"Anne, are you here?" Priscilla called out from outside the bathroom.

Shit. Why is she in my room?

"I'm in the bathroom, Mom!" Anne shouted. "I'll come out later."

Priscilla knocked on the bathroom door, but before Anne could tell her to go away, Priscilla stepped in.

"Mom! I'm in the tub," Anne scolded.

"And so? There's nothing there that I haven't seen."

Anne rolled her eyes.

Do you want to see my Brazilian wax?

"Helen is cleaning your luggage. Are you going away sometime?" Priscilla asked.

Anne avoided her eyes. "I'm going out of town with the girls this weekend."

"Oh, okay." Priscilla paused and then took a step back. "Well . . . enjoy your bath then."

"Thanks."

"Save some of that candle for me? I love the scent." Her mother grinned at her, and Anne could not help but smile back.

"Okay."

She wanted to tell her mother where she got the candles but decided against it. When she would leave home in a week to live with Daniel, what niceties would come out of this would be for nothing.

But . . . damn you, Laine Geronimo!

"M-Mom?" Anne called out just when her mother turned around.

Priscilla faced her daughter. "Yes, dear?"

"I wanted to say that even though I don't like what you did to Daniel—it was unfair and disrespectful toward him—I understand that parents sometimes do drastic things for their children . . ."

Priscilla stared at her youngest daughter and nodded.

"B-but I'm grown up now. And . . . I make the decisions in my life. If I have to make choices—even difficult ones—I have to, because, well, because . . ." Anne sighed. "I gotta own my life."

Priscilla nodded yet again. "Dear, I . . . yes, I understand what you mean." She heaved a sigh and looked at the ceiling.

"If you feel that I'm not mature enough to make my own decisions because I still live under your roof . . ." Anne took a deep breath and jutted her chin out. "I can be more responsible and find my own place."

There, I've said it. I've said something, so it should be fine that I leave sometime. I can leave and be with Daniel.

Priscilla's head snapped down, and her eyes widened. "Anne, your living here has never been an issue. It never will be." She shook her head. "This is your home just as much as it is mine, just as much as it is your father's."

Anne nodded and stared at the bubbles in the tub.

"Don't leave just because of this. Whether you're old and grey, or you have kids . . . have gotten married, this is always your home," Priscilla assured her. "You understand?"

"O-okay. Thanks, Mom."

Priscilla stared at her daughter, while Anne continued to study the foam on the bath. After a while, Anne heard Priscilla sniffle and leave.

CHAPTER TWENTY-SIX

The Day before the Wedding

Zara walked out the lift of the Crystalline. She was on her way to meet the girls at a fruit shake bar by the beach.

Crystalline, the resort that she was covering in Boracay for the weekend, was a boutique hotel resort in the middle of Station 1 and opened only three months ago. She had flown in the night before because the resort manager wanted her to stay for three days. The resort manager arranged for her to tour all the types of rooms they had available and to dine buffet style at the restaurant for breakfast, lunch, and dinner.

She stopped in her tracks when she saw Matt sitting at the resort lobby, fidgeting with his mobile. He donned a tank and board shorts.

Am I imagining him?

Her mouth fell open, and she walked up to him.

"Matthew Villanueva, don't tell me Don asked you to back me up again." She put her hands on her hips.

He looked at her from head to toe and smiled. She was dressed in a short green crochet-knit beach dress, with her bikini underneath. "Wow." He licked his lips. "You look stunning."

Suddenly realizing that he might be on a personal trip, she shook her head and softened her tone. "Are you here with somebody? I mean, are you here on vacation?"

"Yeah, I came with a couple of friends." He nodded.

"Oh, okay." She looked around. "Are you waiting for them?"

"Uh, yeah." He scratched the back of his head. "They might be at the beach already." He cleared his throat. "I was just passing by this area and thought . . . that's a nice-looking hotel . . . You want to hang out?"

"Ha-hang out?" she stammered.

"Well, usually it means walking by the beach, swimming . . . maybe singing at a videoke bar?" he teased her and was rewarded with a smile. "Until . . . I find Euly and Axel again, that is. Those two just keep getting lost . . ."

"If they're together and you're by yourself, don't you think maybe *you're* lost?"

"Yeah . . . maybe." He chuckled.

"Were you waiting . . ." She looked around the lobby and shook her head.

No. Don't be delusional.

But when she looked up at him again, he cleared his throat. "I did kind of . . . drag them down here." He grinned impishly. "Thought it'd be harder for you to turn me away?"

She could not stop the smile and the blush on her cheeks, and she had to look away from him. Throughout their coffee breaks and a few lunches together during the weekdays, she managed to act as if she were only socializing with a colleague.

But in Boracay?

He touched her chin for a moment. "Is it okay if I join you for a while?"

She nodded. "That'd be okay."

He grinned. "Where are you off to this afternoon?"

"Are you two . . . working together again?" Laine asked

when Matt and Zara walked to their table in the fruit shake bar.

The fruit shake bar started as a small joint along the beach but had grown over the years as it became popular among the tourists. The space had been extended since the last time the girls were there, and even though it was not summer season yet, the place was packed. The wall behind the counter had pictures of the owner posing with celebrities holding up their fruit shakes.

"No," Zara answered.

Before she could explain any further, Anne quipped, "Are you two . . . together?"

Zara threw warning glances her way. "He was in the area. He just wanted to hang out."

"What does that mean?" Anne frowned.

Zara pulled Matt toward the bar, throwing Anne a death glare over her shoulder. "Come, let's get a fruit shake."

Matt stopped her. "Let me get the shakes. Which one do you want?"

"Can you get me a ripe mango shake please?"

She reached for her wallet, but Matt walked off before she could take out a bill. She blew out a breath and shook her head.

I'm going to have a panic attack soon!

When she sat down, the other girls stared at her with wide eyes.

"Is there something you want to share with us?" Jazmine finally asked.

"If there was, I'm still figuring it out. I don't like getting involved with somebody from work. He's starting to be all hot in my mind though," Zara confessed and rubbed her temples.

The other three girls giggled.

After a while, Daniel, with Helen and Liam in tow, joined them. Daniel had fetched them from the hotel after Liam woke up. Jazmine stood up to take Liam.

"Hon, this is Matt, Zara's boyfriend," Anne introduced Matt.

Zara choked on her fruit shake, while Laine chuckled. Matt just smiled and shook hands with Daniel.

"Work friend," Zara corrected.

"I just learned about tomorrow," Matt said. "All the best, man."

"Thanks." Daniel smiled back.

Zara frowned when she noticed that Daniel's white piña collared shirt was dampened at the back and chest.

Daniel placed his arm around Anne and said, "I have to go meet Ronnie at the hotel, or make sure that he finds it."

Anne giggled and laid a palm on Daniel's chest. "But I thought he was coming later?"

Daniel nodded, his eyes roaming the bar. "I asked him to take an earlier flight."

"Okay. The girls and I will be getting massages by the beach. You know the place with the *manangs*,[28] right?"

She motioned in the direction of where they would be heading soon.

"Yep." He gave her a clumsy kiss on the forehead, waved goodbye to the rest, and left.

"He'll be all mine soon," Anne muttered purposefully. "Just one more night."

They all shook their heads at her.

"And that's why we don't want to stay anywhere near your hotel," Jazmine quipped. When Anne turned to bat her on the head, she shielded herself.

"He's been so busy here in Boracay. Always running

---

[28] A salutation that refers to women who are older in age, used as a sign of respect

around, doing errands and what-not." Anne rolled her eyes. "I keep telling him that Zara has it all planned out."

Zara leaned forward. "What *is* he taking care of?"

Anne merely shrugged and took a sip from her fruit shake.

"I can't believe you're getting married." Laine hugged Anne close. "The spitfire among us will be chained to her man forever. Dun-dun-dun-dun!"

"I hope it'll be more like chained to the bed," Anne joked back.

All the girls made a face. Matt tried to laugh as silently as he could to himself.

"Okay, time check. Anne, we have thirty minutes before our group spa," Zara announced as she browsed through the schedule in her mobile. "Then, after that, you're scheduled for a manicure and pedicure back at your hotel. You should be able to make it in time if you get just a ninety-minute massage."

Matt gawked at her. "Are you seriously like this even on vacation?"

The three other girls laughed.

"Thanks, Zara. We really couldn't have pulled this off with a couple of weeks' notice without you. You know I'm just teasing you." Anne turned to Matt. "Matt, please join us tomorrow."

"I'm afraid that I'd be intruding on something really private." Matt glanced around the beach. "Plus, my bandmates might say I bailed on them . . ."

"Oh no, no. A friend of Zara's is a friend of ours." Anne shook her head and smiled at Zara like a Cheshire cat.

"If you're sure . . ." Matt smiled. "Thanks."

Then Matt slid his arm around Zara's shoulders and pulled her to him. She heated up when their bodies touched. Bringing his lips close to her ear, he whispered, "The OCD is ridiculous but still very endearing."

Zara glowered at him. "You mention OCD again, and I'm uninviting you from the wedding!"

He drew her closer. Looking at her in the face, he smiled and brushed his hand over her hair. She looked into his eyes and softened.

"We'll be leaving in a while for the massage. Want to get one too?" she asked.

"Nah, I think I really have to go find the guys now." He chuckled, continuing to touch her hair. "They just texted me about going to Puka Beach."

Zara nodded. "If you find some time later . . . maybe you can join us for dinner?"

"Was hoping you'd say something." He chuckled. "If your group won't mind, that is. Just let me know what time to meet you and where."

"Laine, where are we going for dinner again?" Zara turned to Laine and was surprised to find the girls gaping at her and Matt. Even Helen was grinning at her from ear to ear. "What?"

Laine quickly recovered. "We're going to the new ribs restaurant Grill'd at Station 2. The reviews were very positive. And apparently they have great lemongrass martinis."

Matt nodded and then bade the girls goodbye.

After finishing their fruit shakes, they all headed for the *manangs*, who stayed under the shade of coconut palms. People were to lie down on the mats laid out under the palms, and the *manangs* would give massages right there. Privacy was thrown to the wind, but the women were skilled, and the price even better.

"I have to breastfeed Liam first. You girls go ahead, okay?" After checking that there were no loosely hanging coconuts,

205

Jazmine went to sit at the root of a palm.

Helen helped her settle down with a nursing cover, and Liam took his fill. The three other girls went to get their beauty treatments.

After breastfeeding, Jazmine laid a blanket on the sand and placed Liam in the middle. He was learning to lift his head nowadays. Helen sat across her and teased Liam with a stuffed lion toy. Jazmine took out the toy pail and shovel she bought the other week for this trip.

"It's his first time at the beach," Jazmine said.

"From what I heard, he could've been born on a beach," Helen quipped and smiled broadly.

Jazmine laughed. "Please don't remind me about that."

Jazmine cupped some sand in her right hand and brought it near Liam's hand, wondering if he would like the texture. When the sand reached his hand, Liam stopped moving for a while, then began feeling the grains with his fingers and palm. She gasped in delight. He smiled, and saliva dripped down his chin, which made Jazmine giggle.

Suddenly, a gust of wind blew their way, and some sand flew right onto Liam's face.

Jazmine gasped. "There's sand in his mouth!"

She scrambled to get the wipes from her bag.

"Here, let me get that," Helen offered and held out the dispenser.

"Ack! He's getting sand in his eyes!"

Jazmine snatched several wipes from the dispenser and padded them over Liam's face.

She turned to Helen, scrunching her face, and asked, "Should we bring him to a hospital?"

Helen burst out in laughter and shook her head.

"Ms. Jaz, he'll cry soon enough, and the sand will come off

his eyes," Helen assured her, patting a hand over Jazmine's arm.

As Jazmine hesitated and peered down at her son, Helen grinned and stared out at the finest beach she had ever seen. She had never been there before. If it was not for Liam, she would still be wondering why everybody fancied Boracay. Now she knew why. It was a place where expectations were satisfied and more, romance was kindled, and friendships were fused ever more tightly.

CHAPTER TWENTY-SEVEN

Anne and Daniel

Anne fixed an imaginary crease on the white dress that was laid on her bed. It was a strapless couture dress with frills on the bodice, a short flowing bottom, and a long lacy trail at the back that touched her ankles. She smiled at it and then appraised her hotel room. The white walls were spotless and decorated with abstract paintings in gold-colored frames. The queen-size bed was perched on top of a bronze-finished wooden platform. The glass walls, showcasing a view of the sea, were adorned by ecru curtains and white sheer drapes. It was perfect for a bride-to-be.

She could not help thinking about the look on her parents' faces when she tells them that she got hitched. She shook her head to chase the thought away. This day should be about only her and Daniel. Her parents had nothing to do with it.

Somebody knocked on her door. Checking the peephole first, she gasped when she saw that it was Daniel.

"Babe, it's bad luck to see each other before the wedding," she called out from inside the room, but she smiled.

He must want to look at me and hold me now.

"Anne, uh, I need to talk to you."

"Babe . . . has something happened? Are you okay?"

He looked flustered and was sweating and red on the face. He also avoided her eyes.

"I need to talk to you. Can I come in?"

He peered inside, checking if anybody else were there. She opened the door. He turned to her when she closed it behind them, but he looked only at his hands.

"Anne, I don't think we should do this," he rasped.

She shook her head. "Is it because of my parents? That this will destroy my relationship with them? I've sounded off leaving the house to Mom, though not fully and not directly . . . But it should be fine, hon."

"No. I haven't been up-front with you on why I'm not in good terms with my family anymore."

He pinched the bridge of his nose.

"So it's because of you and your family?" she asked.

"Anne, my parents and I don't get along . . . But in order for that to happen, I-I . . ." He paused as his body tensed. "I-I was in a gay relationship before."

She took a deep breath. "Okaaay." She hesitated and shook her head. "W-what are you telling me? Are you trying to make sure I'm okay with your past?" She swallowed. "That doesn't seem to change anything if . . . we love each other and are committed to each other now."

Right? Right?

"Anne, I adore you, and I think you're the most beautiful girl."

She started to smile.

He's just having cold feet.

"But now . . . I-I have to accept that I'm more inclined toward men. More so than I could ever be . . . toward women."

Her eyes rolled back in her head.

"What?" she hissed, and her head snapped forward at him. She could not tell if she were shocked or angry or both. "Why are you saying this to me now?"

"An ex-boyfriend of mine has been trying to get me back the past month. You and I are in a committed relationship, and I've been telling him not to screw with my mind." He drew a sharp breath. "But I can't—he means a lot to me." He looked at her, his eyes wide with desperation.

"So what you're really telling me is that you're in love with someone else?" she snapped. Her heart began to pound like a war boat's drums, and her head spun.

"God. It sounds like I've been cheating on you." He looked around the room, willing for an answer to come to him. "That I lied to you. God, I did lie to you. I kept this from you. And now that I'm trying to accept this about me with more surety, I-I'm dragging you into a pit. You must know . . . I've never been in love with another woman more than with you."

"H-how can this be true? We made love. You kissed me like . . . like you wanted me!"

Anne clenched her fists. Her mind played back the scenes of their time together—their kisses and the sex, the way he would close his eyes and grunt as they made out, how they made love only once each time they were together.

"I did want you. I . . . It's difficult to explain."

Her head snapped up. "Try me!"

"The-there's just a part of me that I know will keep asking what if. If we get married . . . then later, what if . . . what if . . ." He shook his head and wiped his brow.

No, no, no!

She clutched at his shirt. "Daniel, please. You're a man. We're great together. I love you. You love me. Remember?"

"But you and Zack . . . that's irreplaceable too. I thought . . ." His eyes widened as he studied her expression.

She glowered at him. "What thing with Zack?"

"That you . . ." He gestured with his right hand, waving it in

210

the air. "That he . . ."

She demanded, "What? Were you hoping that there was something between Zack and me? So that, so that we can cancel this wedding?"

Daniel covered his face, and Anne's body shook.

Oh my God. He's fucking serious!

"Then why did you agree to all this?" she screamed, gesturing to her dress. Her eyes watered.

"Because I do love you. You were crying when you came to me that night. You asked me to marry you . . . You looked so beautiful through your tears, and I couldn't stand to see you cry."

"You son of a bitch! Don't you dare blame this all on me."

"I'm not—"

She growled and raised a hand to slap him in the face. He drew a sharp breath and dove out of the way.

"Anne, please," he begged.

Suddenly, there was a knock at the door, and it opened. Laine, still carrying her snorkel and mask from a dive that morning, stepped in. Zara came in after her.

"He wants to be with somebody else! His ex-boyfriend!" Anne screamed as she pointed a finger at Daniel. "So he's leaving me! On our wedding day! You son of a bitch!"

Daniel looked like he wanted to run from the room. He turned his eyes to the two by the door and pleaded, but they would not budge.

"We're not moving away unless Anne says so." Zara glared at him.

Daniel cursed.

"Is this what my parents found out about you?" Anne screamed.

"It might've been. I don't know."

A guttural roar came from Anne, which made everybody in the room jump. She pulled back her arm and landed a purposeful punch right on his gut. He grunted in pain and shielded his body. She glared at the cowering man and then suddenly took a deep breath and broke out in sobs. Laine ran to her and hugged her, soothing her and brushing her hair.

Zara softened when she saw the look on Daniel's face—embarrassment at having had an audience and anguish for breaking the heart of a woman.

"Daniel, can you please leave now?" Zara requested.

Daniel shuffled out the room.

"He led me on! He led me on!" Anne wailed in between sobs. She collapsed on the floor and tried to catch her breath.

Zara rushed to get a wet face towel from the bathroom and came back with it and a box of tissues. She knelt beside Anne and wiped her face.

"Anne, sometimes the heart is a complicated, confusing thing." Laine searched her mind for all the positive things she could say. "It's better that you know now than later."

"You're the prettiest woman a guy can ever have," Zara added and frowned.

"You swear? There's nothing wrong with me?" Anne asked Zara.

"Yes, honey. You're the most vibrant, exciting woman there is."

"Yes, I totally agree." Laine smiled at Anne.

Anne looked up at them, sniffing, and then gasped. "My parents should never know that we planned to get married."

Both girls nodded.

"They're going to ask about him. I'll . . . I'll just tell them that I got bored with him. That's believable, right?"

Zara and Laine nodded again and offered her another tissue.

"I was going to move in with him this week. I imagined us spending many nights just holed up in his apartment." Anne sobbed again.

Zara muttered, "I don't understand this. I thought he was becoming possessive of you."

"I still remember the first time we met at that bar," Anne rambled on. "He was so handsome when he walked up to our group and said hi. He said hi while he was looking at me with that kind of look. That kind of look that says he's interested, you know? That look that makes you . . . sizzle, you know?" She turned to her listeners, with a wild look in her eyes. They nodded, not daring to argue with her at the moment. "I thought that he looked so sexy and that we had such good chemistry. All this time he never really wanted me. All this time I was just dreaming and being stupid. Oh my God, I'm an *ilusyonada*!"[29] she wailed and cried another bucket of tears.

Suddenly, Jazmine stepped into the room.

"What are you guys up to?" Jazmine asked when she saw them. "You gals okay?"

Anne was all too eager to fill her in. For another two emotional hours, she went over the events that transpired that afternoon again and again, sobbing in between details, blowing her nose after crying, and screaming into a pillow at times.

Everybody was sprawled on the bed. Anne was drained.

Suddenly Zara gasped when the practicalities of the matter dawned on her. "Oh my gosh. I have to cancel with the officiator."

She stood up, walked out of the room, and made the phone calls.

---

[29] A woman who is delusional

Anne groaned as she surveyed the room, "I'm so sorry I dragged you all the way here for nothing."

"We were having fun . . . until a few hours ago, of course. The weather has never been better. Do you maybe want to go and hang out under the sun?" Laine suggested.

"I'm still in shock. I can't believe this happened," Jazmine spoke up. "I kept preparing myself for after the wedding. That this—"

"What did I miss? How did I never see this coming?" Anne groaned and sprawled her body on the floor. "He had mentioned an ex-girlfriend! A Kristelle! Do you think . . . do you think I'll ever get to this point again with another guy? Maybe I should join the nunnery . . ." She sat up. "Laine! You and I should!"

"Anne, I've never considered becoming a nun." Laine made a face at the suggestion. "If it'll make you feel better, we can go lounge by the beach?"

Anne, aghast, stared at her but then softened. "Chocolate fudge cake?"

"Yes, plus mangoes."

"Green mangoes with *bagoong*?"[30] Anne's eyes widened with want.

"Yes!"

Anne wiped her eyes and lumbered to the bathroom.

Laine shook her head at Jazmine. "This is awful! And last week we were just bumming about this wedding. This is horrible, horrible, horrible."

By the time Anne stepped out of the bathroom, Zara had made the cancellations, and Jazmine had tidied up the mess. Laine put her arm around Anne and kissed her on the cheek.

---

[30] A Philippine condiment made of partially or completely fermented fish or krill and salt

"The sea will make you feel better."

CHAPTER TWENTY-EIGHT

Salvage Some

Anne stood up and announced, "We have to break into Daniel's hotel room."

Zara and Laine groaned. They were lying down on lounge chairs by the beach and staring at the people walking by, getting on Jet Skis, and boarding *paraws*.[31] Jazmine took another bite of the green mango slice in her hand.

Zara admonished, "Can we please put an end to this break-in business?"

"No. I-I need to go in. There's something I need to get back. And I really, really need to," Anne insisted. Her eyebrows furrowed, and she mulled over the situation.

"I'm willing to go with you, if you need to do this," Jazmine offered and sat up.

Anne paced the length of her plastic chair and back.

"What is it, Anne? Is it really that important?" Zara pried.

"Yes. Yes, it's vital that I get it—them." Anne stopped in her tracks and placed her hands on her hips.

Zara frowned. "What did you leave behind? Jewelry?" Her eyes widened. "Underwear?"

"No." Anne frowned. "It's much worse than that."

Zara sat up. "What is it? If we're going to break in, we

---

[31] A double outrigger sailboat native to the Visayas region of the Philippines

216

should know at least what we're risking our heads for."

Laine faced Anne. "What if you just tell Daniel that you left some stuff in his room and that you need to get them? And can he please not be around while you're there?"

The three other girls stared at Laine for a while.

Zara clapped her hands. "That'll work. I'm for that."

Jazmine chuckled.

Anne turned the doorknob. The door was unlocked, just as Daniel told Laine he would leave it. When Anne stepped into the room though, she froze in her tracks. A king-size bed was in the middle of the room—four boudoir pillows, encased in silver embroidered silk shams, leaned back against the sleeping pillows that lay below the charcoal-colored tufted headboard. A rayon throw lined the end of the bed, and matching ruffles hung from the bed's boxspring to the floor. Images of what she had, before this weekend, imagined happening between her and Daniel filled her mind.

Suddenly, Jazmine bumped against her from behind.

No time to waste. I must salvage what's left of my pride.

Anne broke out of her traitorous reverie and walked into the room. Zara followed after Jazmine, then Laine.

"Okay. First, let's take all his clothes, dump them in the bathtub, and fill it to the brim," Jazmine piped up.

"No, no." Anne sighed. "I-I just need his laptop . . . and any hard drives you might find."

Zara stiffened. "Please don't tell me we're here to do what I think we're about to do."

Anne looked into Zara's eyes. "I'm afraid you might already know what I need to do."

Laine frowned. "What's in his laptop? Some confidential information? You brought work with you when you were at his

217

place?"

Jazmine walked over to the desk by the window. "Family business stuff?"

Zara pursed her lips and headed for the luggage by the cabinet. Laine opened the bedside table's drawers and peeked in. Anne sat down on the bed, with her shoulders slumped. She watched as her friends searched the room.

If there is any categorically demoralizing moment in my life, this would be fucking it.

"I found his laptop," Zara announced as she took out a bursting sleeve from Daniel's suitcase. "There doesn't seem to be any hard drives in here."

"There's a USB stick here on the table," Jazmine announced, waving the gadget in the air.

"Nothing here," Laine spoke up and walked to Jazmine's side by the table.

Zara brought the MacBook to the table and turned it on. "Anne, we need a password."

Anne huffed out a breath and lay down on the bed. "It's daniel123. All lowercase."

When the desktop screen came to view, Zara called out to Anne, "We're in."

Anne dragged herself to the table and sat on the swiveling chair. After taking a deep breath, she opened the Images folder, and pictures of her and Daniel's beaming faces popped up. Laine gasped.

Laine implored, "Please tell me you're not erasing all your memories."

Anne selected all the pictures and was about to press Delete, when she sighed and pressed Escape. She whimpered, "We looked happy, didn't we?"

Laine placed a hand on Anne's shoulders. "I hate to say it,

but you guys looked great together." She sighed.

Jazmine watched from over Anne's other shoulder. Zara stepped away and sat on the bed.

This time, Anne selected the Videos folder.

"Hey, that's the two of you at the beach yesterday," Laine pointed out and peered closer at the thumbnails.

When Anne scrolled down the folder, Laine squealed and took a step back. "Anne Tioleco!" Her hands flew to her mouth. "Is that Daniel? Naked?"

Jazmine's eyes widened, and she took a closer look. "Yep. And that's Anne naked too." She held up her hands in front of her and headed for the bed. "Okay. This, I don't want to see."

Laine scurried away too, while Anne scrolled farther down the folder. She searched for that first video she and Daniel had ever taken. He had taken her to Café Havana one night, on the first month they dated. They had taken a video of themselves dancing together and made faces at the phone. She sniffled. She selected the rest of the videos and deleted them, but she saved her favorite one for him.

Oh God. Here come the waterworks again.

From the corner of her eyes, she saw her friends throw her worried looks.

As she shut the laptop down, her eyes landed on the topmost side drawer of the desk. It was partially opened, and she could see a black pouch inside. She sucked in a breath and nervously reached for it. In the pouch were two familiar black boxes. She opened the one with her name on it, and her whole body froze when she saw the two rings inside. She could not breathe just then.

When she and Daniel went to a jewelry shop the previous week to search for their wedding bands, it had been easy to select the ring for Daniel, but there were too many options for

Anne. Finally, they shortlisted two choices: a three-tone gold ring set with diamonds all around, which Daniel favored the most, and a pink gold ring set with three diamonds, which Anne liked the best. In the end, she had given in because he insisted on getting the more expensive one for his bride-to-be. Little did she know that he bought both rings.

"Anne, are you okay? What did you find?" Jazmine asked.

Anne remained on the chair as she marveled at the rings.

"Anne, what did you find?" Laine pried.

Zara cursed when she saw what was in Anne's hands. Laine and Jazmine grabbed each other's hand as they braced themselves for Anne to break down again.

"He bought two rings for me," Anne whispered, more to herself than to the others.

Zara sat down beside her and peered closer. The rings were beautiful, but she did not dare say it. She slid her arm around Anne's shoulders.

"He loved you," Zara said matter-of-factly.

"I suppose . . . ," Anne breathed.

"He didn't mean to hurt you, Anne."

"I know," she whispered.

"Sometimes, the past just catches up with us." Zara squeezed her shoulders and let go, afraid to set off her emotions.

But then Anne held on to Zara and sobbed. The girls frowned, but they were relieved her sobs seemed less anguished.

After she put the rings back in the drawer, Anne asked, "Can we go now?"

It took her a while to regain her composure again, but now she wanted to leave more than anything else. The place was a stark reminder of what could have been.

Her three friends nodded but said nothing.

"I need some whisky," Anne grumbled as she pulled down her sunglasses to cover her bloodshot eyes. "Can we go diving tomorrow? Maybe that will make this trip worthwhile."

All the girls soundly said yes.

"Hold on," Jazmine called out.

Jazmine wrapped her arms around Anne and Laine, pulling them in for a huddle. Zara joined them, pressing her forehead against Jazmine's. Anne laid her head on Jazmine's shoulder, and Laine leaned against Zara.

"This isn't the end of us. Our falls don't define us. We are strong because we have each other," Jazmine declared.

They took deep breaths together.

CHAPTER TWENTY-NINE
What Lies Ahead

That night, the girls and Matt hit a lounge bar on the beach. Plush beanbags and low tables were scattered about the sand in front of the bar. An acoustic band played chill and reggae songs. Before Zara could sit down on one of the beanbags, Matt tugged her by the hand.

"Let's dance." He motioned his head to the spot below the platform, where a few people swayed to the beat and waved their hands in the air.

"What? No, I've never danced here before."

"It's going to be fine."

He tugged at her again, this time gripping her wrist. As he pulled her, she glanced back at her friends with a defeated look on her face. They grinned at her like Cheshire cats.

When they had joined the crowd, Matt danced, mimicking the dorky dance moves of Jean-Claude van Damme in *Kickboxer*.

Zara doubled over in laughter, almost snorting. She grabbed his arms and tried to keep them down. "Stop it! Stop it!"

He chuckled and swayed to the beat, motioning her to dance too. "Are you embarrassed to be seen with me?"

She shook her head and laughed. "No, I'm embarrassed by your dancing." She looked him in the eyes. "I don't think anybody could be embarrassed to be . . . seen with you . . ."

She cleared her throat and asked, trying for light conversation, "What kind of music does your band play?"

Matt slid his arms around her waist and moved her close to him. She shivered. She loved being in the arms of a man she admired in the workplace and outside of it. That he had a handsome face and smiling eyes, a boyish kind of look, with a lean, muscled body to match, was the irresistible icing on the cake.

"Rock," he answered. "Mostly ballads."

"How come I've never heard that about you?"

"Well, I only invite the guys from work to come watch a gig. They usually don't rat me out."

"You've heard me sing before. You should sing to me sometime so that we're even," she teased.

Matt brought his lips to her ear and began to sing alongside the band's vocalist. "Was I out of my head? Was I out of my mind? How could I have ever been so blind?"

His singing voice was deeper and smoother than his usual. It was all that she could hear amid the crowd; it weighed her down, made her melt, made her want to wrap her arms around his neck and run her fingers through his hair. Her heart began to beat faster. His breath on her ear was bringing her closer to her wits' end.

Suddenly Matt leaned in and gave her a kiss on the lips. He felt Zara freeze in his arms. He pulled his head back and cursed.

"Sorry about that."

She relaxed and smiled. He held her closer and tried for another kiss, but she pulled back.

"Matt, I like you, but I've just been out of a rela—," she murmured.

"I know. I heard." He shook his head, cursing the island for making him want her even more than he did when they were in Manila.

"A-at the same time, I'm scared . . . but I like you." She looked up at him with doe-like eyes, searching his for any signs of insincerity.

He smiled, pleased. "That's definitely better than you saying you have a rule against getting involved with people at work."

"Actually, I do have that rule." She chuckled. "Which I just conveniently forgot about . . ."

"I'm not rushing anything. I just . . . I think about you all the time. You keep distracting me when I'm working . . ." He chuckled.

She grinned, nodded, and took a deep breath. She grabbed the chance to brush her fingers across his cheek. She had wanted to do that since they had their first cup of coffee together.

He'll drop me once he finds out I'm a bit neurotic. Shoot, shoot, shoot.

Before he could smile down at her, she tiptoed to kiss him on the lips. After savoring the feel of his lips on hers, she turned around and tugged him away from the crowd.

"Come, let's go back to my friends before I break any more of my rules."

Anne was on her third glass of whisky now, not counting those she had in the afternoon. She wanted to get wasted, to forget about the heartbreak and the humiliation. When she felt her mind drift, she went to the lounge chair beside Laine's beanbag and lay down. Whisky was her lover for the night.

Laine's mobile suddenly beeped as she took a big gulp from her coconut milkshake.

Tony:	I'm leaving Bohol tonight. Had to move my flight to Virginia back earlier. Work reasons.
Laine:	Wow. So soon?
Tony:	Yep. It was nice to see you. I'll look you up online.
Laine:	Okay. Have a safe flight.

Her heart sank. It was the closest she had ever been to falling in love. She supposed some things were just not meant for her. She was meant to trudge through life with her girlfriends, social work, and conservation outreaches. She shivered when she remembered the dream she had the other night. In it, Tony had surprised her at Boracay and wooed her. He told her he would not stop pursuing her until she agrees to have him. She sighed ruefully as she recalled his kisses, his embrace . . . She probably had to do more than save a *dugong* to get her romantic happily ever after.

Jazmine glanced at her watch a tenth time. She wanted to be the one to put Liam to sleep this night. She worried that he might look for her and get upset when he finds she is not around. Her mind battled between being there for Anne, who was starting to snooze away at the lounge chair, and being there for her son.

Hypothetically, Anne should be asleep in ten minutes. Liam would want to fall asleep in twenty minutes. That gives me enough time to walk back to the resort after Anne falls asleep.

She checked every few minutes if Anne had already dozed off. Her friends meant the world to her, even more now than before, but her son meant the universe.

Zara glanced at her friends. How was it that when their hearts were breaking, hers was being kindled yet again? She looked at the man sharing a couple's beanbag with her as he nodded his head to the band's music. His one hand tapped his knee to the beat while the other held hers. By his grip, it seemed that he would not let her go, at least for the evening. She smiled and dared to lean her head on his shoulder. He halted the tapping and then slipped his arm around her shoulders. She leaned back, tucked her legs under her knees, and stared out at the sea ahead, upon which the full moon's light danced.

CHAPTER THIRTY

Girlfriends Make It All Good

"Great morning!" Laine beamed at the sea around them.

The four of them boarded the diving boat that afternoon, along with another party of four people, and now headed for the second dive site. Diving was the one thing Laine did that was thrilling and was probably even a little scary. It was an indulgence, but she felt it was honorable to love the sea. When she met new people and had to make small talk, chatting about diving often intrigued them about her.

Anne groaned. It was her idea to go diving today, but instead of being the one to steer her friends into the fun, she was the last one to get out of bed and grumbled all throughout breakfast, lunch, and the trip. She had busted her butt to leave her hotel room though because it was their last day in Boracay. She was just grateful she had fallen asleep on the beanbag the other night, before she could drink herself to a morning hangover.

Jazmine yawned and stretched on the stern of the boat. Liam had woken up at five o'clock that morning, and by the time he fell back to sleep, she was too wide awake to sleep again. She was not a certified diver like the other girls, and she was only there that afternoon for the boat ride. She put on her sunglasses, thinking she could get some shut-eye when the girls were back in the water. Or maybe she could just read a few pages of the romance book she had tucked away in her beach bag. When Braden left her, she had vowed off romance, but now she does not want to give up on it. Not yet. She would give it another chance, but maybe just *one* more.

Zara grumbled when she could not find her sunglasses in her beach bag. She must have left it at her room. She had tossed and turned in her bed most of the previous night because Matt kept assaulting her thoughts. It seemed early for her to consider dating again.

And somebody from the office! But he is somebody . . . awesome in the office. And outside it . . . Argh, no!

Every time she thought about him, she ended up with a stupid grin on her face. She would then shake her head, trying to push thoughts of him away, but the man just would not leave her mind! It took a lot of effort from her this morning not to invite him to go diving with them, but she did not want to put Anne off by letting a guy tag along. The diving party was still pretty antitestosterone this morning.

"Okay, we're here!" Timmy, the dive guide, motioned the boatman to slow down the boat.

They were about a hundred meters away from the nearest island. The guide showed them a map of the area and talked about the route they would take and what they might see there. The entire party except Jazmine hung on to his every word, hoping he would mention an underwater marvel they had not seen before.

When the guide dropped into the water, all geared up, the rest of the group followed suit. Jazmine waved at her friends before they descended. Then she lay down on the boat and dozed off.

The divers drifted with little effort underwater and could see sixty meters ahead. Laine and Zara buddied up, while Anne partnered with the guide. The other party broke up into pairs. Laine, Zara, and Anne were all experienced divers though, so the guide left the three of them to loiter around, only tapping on his tank to call them when it was time to move on.

They arrived at the highlight of the dive site, which was a huge reef that was home to families and families of corals, hard and soft alike, and anemones. Laine spotted a bunch of tube corals that housed batfishes inside them. She gestured for Anne and Zara to take a look. Zara spotted a hole with a lobster inside. She extended her dive stick near it, and it snapped its larger pincer at the stick, sending a strong vibration through her hand.

After seeing what the other girls had spotted, Anne ventured toward the top of the reef. She was rewarded for getting out of bed that day. From the top, one had a good view of the twenty-meter-long reef and the vivid colors that emblazoned it. Groups of fishes moved about together on top of the corals left and right. Half-meter-long lionfishes lurked close to the reef. Hard corals sprang their bodies outward into the water. Sea fans danced to the current of the sea. After taking in the sight, she looked about her and found nudibranchs, decked in different neon colors, on a brain coral. She reached out to lay one of them on her palm.

Velvety and squishy.

When she reached the end of the reef, there was nothing beyond it but a wide stretch of sand. As she hovered in the water, a shadow—probably that of a cloud or a boat—passed overhead, and the area dimmed. And suddenly her mind emptied, and emotions seeped in.

All this, it doesn't change the fact that I've just been dumped. At my wedding.

Her face scrunched up. She closed her eyes as they watered. Her breathing quickened through the regulator.

Suddenly somebody held her by the shoulder. It was Zara. Zara peered at her and then frowned. Zara motioned to someone behind them. After a while, Laine joined her two friends.

Laine gestured to Anne, "You, ascend?"

Anne hesitated and then nodded. Laine raised a palm, signaling them to wait. She swam toward Timmy, who was checking the air supply of the other divers. She indicated to him that they wanted to exit the water. Timmy pulled out his map and showed her where they were.

After a minute, he led the three ladies to a spot near the reef. He took out a diver-down flag from his pack, filled it with air, and let the marker surface first. Laine then motioned to Zara and Anne. They followed her lead, advancing up the water. The three girls surfaced. Then Laine pulled out the whistle from her pocket and began to blow hard on it, hoping that the boatman would hear her.

It was not until after a minute more that they heard the sound of a motorboat. It was heading in their direction!

"What happened?" Jazmine asked them when the boat stopped. "I've just slept for ten minutes. And why are you all the way over here?"

Anne sniffed, pulling her body up the side ladder. She plopped herself on the bench.

"We just got tired," Laine explained, stowing their gears

away.

Zara threw Jazmine a warning glance, dipping her head in Anne's direction.

"This weekend is a disaster!" Anne groaned. She peeled her wetsuit from her upper body, leaned back, and covered her face with her palms.

Zara sat down beside Anne and wrapped an arm around her shoulders.

"It was. It really, really sucked," Zara agreed.

Anne managed to blurt out, "Thanks for pulling out the water with me though."

"If you'd gone by yourself, you'd have made all the fish cry," Laine teased.

Anne chuckled as she wiped the back of her hand over her eyes. Jazmine giggled and settled down on the other side of Anne.

"We'd never leave you," Zara vowed.

Suddenly, with an impish smile on her face, Laine jumped up and belted out a song. "I'm . . . I'm so in love with you." She wiggled a finger at Anne, trying to remember the silly wedding dance for Daniel.

"Whatever you want to do," Zara joined in, swaying her hips.

"Is all right with me," Jazmine sang along, raising her hand high over her head and shimmying.

"'Cause you make me feel so brand-new!" the three girls shouted and danced in front of Anne, daring her to join them in song. "And I want to spend my life with you!"

A smile tugged at Anne's lips. Finally, she stood up and, without saying a word, wrapped her arms around her friends. She wanted to cry, she did. But at least she had them to hold on to.

The boat drowned out their singing, but with their heads and hearts together, they only heard each other and the promise of a friendship that would last.

Anne

Anne, wearing a carmine woven gauze V-neck romper, dragged her luggage through the door. She walked down the hallway that would lead to the living room, where she knew she could take a bottle of Johnnie Walker Black Label Scotch whisky from the mahogany bar cabinet and take shot after shot. She could only last eight though.

Or maybe a junk food binge would be better. Then I can watch Breakfast at Tiffany's. *With a bottle of tequila. Yeah, I can last far longer with tequila.*

As she passed by the living room, a movement caught her eye. Priscilla, dressed in a black-and-white Aztec-patterned wrap dress, was looking through the magazine rack that was beside the couch. She looked up just as Anne was about to scamper away.

"Hi, Mom," Anne breathed. "I just came back."

I hope she doesn't notice that my eyes make me look vampy. I should've worn sunglasses.

"Hi, honey." Priscilla smiled and, after grabbing a newspaper, sauntered toward Anne. "How was your trip?"

Anne tensed as Priscilla closed in. "It was good. Had fun. Went diving."

Priscilla kissed Anne on the cheek. "Did all of you girls go diving?"

Priscilla brushed Anne's bangs to the side with her fingers. Anne watched as Priscilla's eyes centered on hers, as her mother's lips tensed in a line, and as her eyebrows furrowed.

Shit!

"W-we all did. Except Jaz." Anne let out a chuckle and a smile. "She really should take diving lessons. She's missing out on a lot."

"Well, diving is expensive and considering Jaz's priorities . . ." Priscilla frowned and looked Anne over. "Was Daniel with you girls?"

"Y-yes, he was." Anne's grip on her baggage tightened. "Umm . . . but Jaz doesn't dive because she has a fear of the water."

"Hmm . . . sometimes people have concerns that they don't want to talk about." Priscilla slid an arm around Anne's shoulders. "So they bring up other things instead."

"Mom," Anne groaned, "please don't talk in riddles. It's much too early in the day."

"I'm not talking in riddles." Priscilla scolded her, "And you just came back from a vacation. Why are you moody?"

"I'm not—" Anne sighed and looked down at the ground. "Just an early morning flight."

I almost gave myself away there.

"Anne . . ." Priscilla nudged her daughter's chin up. "Are you okay?"

Anne continued to stare downward.

Oh God! Don't!

But Anne's lips quivered, and her eyes watered. She sucked in a breath, and the tears fell.

Priscilla held her by the shoulders. "What happened?"

Anne shook her head.

Nothing. Nothing happened. That's the problem.

"Nothing . . . ," Anne breathed.

I can't tell you. It's too embarrassing.

Priscilla pulled Anne to the couch.

"Mom, I don't want to sit down. I don't want to talk about this with you—"

Priscilla grabbed her arm and yanked it down. Anne yelped and wiped her tears away.

"You know, when you were young," Priscilla shared, "you'd cry every time I left the house."

"Really?" Anne grumbled, even though she could remember the fits she threw back then when her mother would say goodbye.

"Yes. When your sisters were about that age, they'd cry too, but you . . . you wouldn't just cry. You'd run after me all the way to the door. When I closed it behind me, I could still hear you kicking at it."

Anne harrumphed.

"I know you still resent your Dad and me for having Daniel investigated, but that's only because . . ." Priscilla took a deep breath. "I feel that you trust people too much, too soon."

"W-what?" Anne murmured.

Priscilla repeated, "I feel that you trust people too much, too soon."

"I don't, Mom." Anne shook her head. "I just take a shot with people."

"I know." Priscilla sighed. "And in that, you leave yourself vulnerable. Because people may hurt you."

"They don't have to be perfect—" Anne choked on her words. "They don't have to be perfect for me to care about them."

"I know. And it's not . . . always a bad thing. I'm just here to look out for you."

Anne frowned at her. "So you were the one who had him investigated?" Anne's eyes widened as she asked, "Dad had nothing to do with it?"

Priscilla heaved a sigh and looked down at the floor. "Y-yes . . . It's not that I don't trust you. I just . . . I'm still a mother. Even though I've let go of looking after your sisters, I can't seem to let go . . . of you yet."

Anne nodded and stared down at the rug.

"I suppose you're still mad if you refuse to talk to me about what happened," Priscilla reckoned. "If you refused to have coffee at Figaro with me last week."

Anne covered her face with her hands and whispered through her fingers, "It didn't work out between Daniel and me." Anne let the tears fall, but her breaths were less hurried now.

Priscilla drew a sharp breath. She wrapped her arms around Anne and patted her on the back. "Hush, honey. Don't let this tear you down." Then in a barely audible whisper, she added, "If I could bear your heartache for you, I would."

Suddenly Raul passed by the hallway. When he saw his wife and youngest daughter in an embrace, he stopped in his tracks and frowned. Priscilla looked up, shook her head, and waved him away. Hesitating, he left them to themselves for the moment.

Jazmine

"Ms. Jazmine, your phone is ringing," Helen called out from the kitchen.

Jazmine giggled as Liam placed his wet lips on hers.

That's gross but sweet.

"Okay. Hold on," Jazmine replied and placed Liam back in the crib.

Maybe it's Tita Fiona.

Jazmine scoffed.

She has no hold on Liam now. Braden's name will be officially removed from Liam's birth certificate in a few weeks.

She jogged to the kitchen and picked up the device vibrating on the counter. When her eyes landed on the screen, she gasped and could not press the answer button any sooner.

"Tin!" Jazmine exclaimed.

Helen glanced at Jazmine, her face a question as she stirred chicken broth on the stove. Jazmine waved a hand to say nothing was wrong. She heard Liam call out to her from the bedroom, but it had been months since she had talked to her sister.

"Ate!" Christine responded.

Jazmine could hear the roar of engines and honks of vehicles from the other end of the line.

"Tin, how are you? I haven't heard from you in a while."

237

Suddenly an ill feeling came to the pit of Jazmine's stomach. "Are Tatay and Nanay okay?"

"Yes, Ate. They're okay," Christine answered. She took a deep breath and said, "Ate, I hope you won't get mad . . ."

"What is it, Tin?" Jazmine pressed.

"I-I'm in Manila now," Christine murmured.

What's she doing here? Did she drop out of school? Is she here for a few days? I can see her!

Jazmine asked, "Why are you here?"

"I-I told Mama that our class has a field trip to Naga for the weekend . . . ," Christine whispered. "Umm . . . I used the money you put in my bank account to come here."

Jazmine tucked the phone between her ear and shoulder, went to her bedroom, and picked out a pair of jeans and a tee from a cabinet.

Christine added, "I promise I didn't tell Mama about the money you kept sending me."

"Where are you right now? Are you staying with me?"

"If you don't mind . . ."

"Of course I don't mind. What are you talking about? Where are you exactly?"

"I'm at the Cubao bus terminal." Christine's voice lifted. "I can take a bus to Mandaluyong."

"Okay. I'll meet you at Jollibee—the one in the Mandaluyong Circle." Jazmine struggled to slip into her jeans while balancing the phone on her neck. "Do you remember it?"

"Yes, Ate. I'm walking to the main road now, to get a ride."

"Okay. The Jollibee with two levels, okay? And ride the bus with the sign that says 'Mandaluyong–Sentro,' not the 'Mandaluyong Road.'"

Christine giggled, and Jazmine relaxed.

"I remember, Ate. Don't worry." Christine paused. "Uh . . . I wanted to see the baby."

"His name is Liam." Jazmine took a deep breath and smiled. "Of course you'll see him. He can't wait to meet his aunt."

Christine sighed. "Okay, Ate. I'll see you in a bit."

"If I get there before you do, shall I order a couple of chocolate sundaes?"

Christine laughed. "They'll melt!"

"You always wait for it to melt." Jazmine rolled her eyes.

The two bickered on about the best temperature ice cream should be in when one ate a serving. Christine giggled yet again, and Jazmine realized how much she missed hearing her sister's voice and laugh. Suddenly that part in her heart that was especially reserved for her family did not seem so empty anymore.

Laine

Michelle, one of Ganoop's facilitators, looked up from her laptop and declared, "We need a mentor on financial literacy to make this project complete." She sighed. "For this to be comprehensive enough to make a difference for these teens."

"That's true. Parents rarely teach their children about money," Grace agreed. "Especially when they don't have enough in their own bank accounts."

Michelle and Laine sat in front of Grace's mahogany desk inside her office. They were called in that morning to update her on the status of their different projects.

"I've tried to get in touch with some professors in different universities. Let me follow up with them in a couple of days," Michelle put in, already on the last topic of the agenda.

"Good. Let me know if anything's turned up by the end of the week," Grace requested. "With all the projects we have on hand, I'm a little wary about taking on a new one. But this new project will increase funding for your areas."

Michelle let out a soft groan, having just reported on eight different projects.

Grace chuckled, holding both her palms up. "I know, I know. I hear you, Michelle." She crossed her arms over her desk and turned to Laine. "I'm not hearing any objections from your end yet, Laine."

Laine glanced at Michelle, who stared at her with wide pleading eyes and pursed lips. Laine looked back at Grace and answered, "What's the project about?"

"Well, the benefactor is interested in sponsoring a series of youth empowerment events. Not just one but several." When Laine merely nodded, Grace continued, "It won't start for another three months, but if the deal pulls through, the program will run for a year."

Laine hesitated for a couple of seconds and then answered, "I-I'll stretch myself."

Grace let out a sigh of relief and beamed. "Good. Laine will take charge of this then." She reached for a black clear folder at the side of her desk. "We'll sort your projects by priority when this one kicks off." She patted the paperwork and warned her staff, "You're going to get busier though."

"I don't mind." Laine paused as she stared at the fresh sheet of paper on her notebook. "I want to get busier."

Michelle raised her eyebrows.

"Great. You'll get busy, but"—Grace grinned—"there's a perk that'll likely come for you."

Michelle leaned forward in her seat.

"The benefactor is abroad," Grace shared. "So there's a big chance you'll get to travel."

Laine's shoulders lifted. "That'd be nice."

Michelle frowned. "Where? Which country?"

Grace finally opened the folder. "The benefactor company is based in Baltimore. In the U.S."

Zara

The four girls were at Laine and Zara's apartment that weekend. Zara and Matt had set camp at the dining table. Papers, photos, and a bag of chips were lying about in front of them. Matt had asked Zara to look over an article he was working on.

Zara said, "Keith's landscape shot is awesome for this," as she lifted up a photo of Mount Pinatubo.

"Yeah. I'm pretty glad Don got someone of his caliber. He's somewhere up there with Oliver," Matt replied.

From the couch, Laine asked Jazmine, "Why don't you ask him now before he can run away?"

"Are you gals talking about Matt?" Zara asked.

He glanced at the girls by the couch.

"Zara and her Vulcan hearing," Anne muttered.

Jazmine took Liam from Laine's lap and walked over to the dining area.

"Matt, can you please hold my son and talk to him?" Jazmine asked him, mustering as much desperation as she could into her eyes.

"What?" he blinked and shook his head.

"Please. There's nobody male present in his life right now. So can you please hold him just for a while? I read that the male touch is very essential to a newborn baby."

"Is this really necessary?" He frowned down at Liam, his eyes wide and his eyebrows raised. He scratched the back of his head and rumpled his hair.

"Yes. Since he only has us girls now, you got to help me. Please, just for a few minutes."

Zara choked and turned red. Anne and Laine peered at Matt in sheer amusement. He looked at the three of them, begging with his eyes for somebody to save him.

Jazmine pleaded some more, "Look at his face and tell me he isn't cute."

Matt cursed. "Zara Castillo, you are so going to owe me for this." Then turning to Jazmine, he held out his hands to get Liam. "I don't even know how to hold a baby. If I drop him, don't tell me I didn't warn you."

"You'll be fine."

Matt tried to balance Liam in his arms.

"I have no idea what I'm doing," he grumbled.

"This is priceless. I've never seen Matthew Villanueva flustered ever." Zara grinned, studying his face.

Matt and Liam stared at each other.

"Can you please say a rhyme or two? Like 'Humpty Dumpty'?" Jazmine requested.

Zara bent over in laughter and earned a glare from Matt.

Then Jazmine pressed again, "Please. I'll bring food the next time you come over."

He considered this for a moment, then said, "I like pizza."

She grinned. "Deal."

When he recited the nursery rhyme, Liam cooed, and the girls craned their necks to watch the man and the baby. Matt then motioned Jazmine to sit beside him. Several rhymes afterward, she was clapping her hands at the coos Liam was making.

When he finished "Jack and Jill," Matt said, "Okay. I think this is getting much too cutesy for me."

The girls laughed but continued to stare at Liam. Zara grinned at Matt as Jazmine took her son and returned to the couch.

"Thanks." Zara chuckled. "Although I think they were really just making fun of you. Liam seems to like you though."

He shrugged at her and said, "I guess, I got the natural charm." He cleared his throat and looked her in the eyes. "It's okay. Whatever it takes to get your friends to like me."

She blinked and quickly turned her gaze down to the table. *Sinking fast . . . Quicksand.*

Zara spread five travel magazines on her office desk the next morning. They were from five different publications—a mix of local and international. She had set some time to read up on the competition. Suddenly tapping came from behind her. Matt stood there, with a notebook tucked under his arm. Her heart picked up a pace, and she looked around to see if anybody glanced their way.

Matt cleared his throat and took a step toward her. She could smell his cologne now, and she wanted to close her eyes and smell the musk and talc.

He leaned forward and whispered, "Coffee in half an hour?"

She snapped back to reality, smiled, and nodded.

"Same place?" He grinned. "You look beautiful by the way."

"Sure. Thanks."

A blush crept up her neck. She had nitpicked at her outfit that morning, spending half an hour looking through her closet and considering pieces. The periwinkle frill Bardot dress accented her slim shoulders, and she had blowdried her hair to let it cascade down in mild waves.

He took her hand in his. "Want to go somewhere this weekend? Maybe drive to Tagaytay? Have a nice lunch?"

The corners of her mouth turned upward. "Hmm . . . fresh air, indulgent food, a handsome date?" she teased. "How can a lady say no?"

He squeezed her hand. Her eyes widened when a faint pink hue touched his cheeks.

Slow down, Zara. You're not ready for this.

He grazed his thumb from the inside of her wrist to the center of her palm.

"The handsome gentleman," he crooned, "will make sure it'll be worth the lady's while."

He made his way to his desk. She watched him, his strides, his easy gait, the muscle of his shoulders, and the strength of his back.

I'm so going to get my heart broken again.

THESSA LIM is a Filipina writer of new adult fiction for women. After growing up in the bustling city of Iloilo, she studied information technology at the Ateneo de Manila University and then worked in Metro Manila before moving to Singapore. Her linguistic repertoire includes Hiligaynon, Bisaya, Tagalog, and English, but she only writes in English (teehee). The Singaporean slang she uses consists of *lah*, *leh*, and *ayo*.

With the *Of Heads and Hearts* series, Thessa wants the world to know about the modern-day Filipina even if it is through light, witty reads.

In her spare time, she reads, takes a dip in the sea, or travels with her family.

To get the latest updates on Thessa and her writing, sign up for her mailing list at www.thessalim.com or follow her Facebook page www.facebook.com/ThessaLimOfficial. Check her out on Instagram at www.instagram.com/thessalim.

www.thessalim.com

www.facebook.com/thessalimofficial

www.instagram.com/thessalim
#OfHeadsandHearts
#OfHeadsandHeartsintheMetro

www.ingramcontent.com/pod-product-compliance
Lightning Source LLC
Chambersburg PA
CBHW031715170626
46808CB00005B/1757